Broken Heels

Chiara Atoyebi

DEDICATION

This book is for my daughter Calais. I was once a little girl
and a young woman too.

ACKNOWLEDGMENTS

To my staff at Vision FromThe Roots. Jide Atoyebi for your continued support and sacrifices. For the many Guardian Angels that made a way for this book to come forth through the toughest of times. To Dionne for pushing me. For my friends that read it in all its stages. For the readers, welcome to my love letter. Thank You.

Broken Heels

CHAPTER ONE

Click, Clack, Click, Clack, Click Clack. Phoenix Mitchell took a couple steps from her hotel in Times Square to the edge of the street. She looked up and smiled as she stared at the gigantic buildings that draped the city's skyline. She breathed a deep sigh of relief. She was finally back in New York City. It was everything she remembered with its fast pace and gritty extravagance, all of which created an electrifying magnetism that she only ever found in Manhattan.

There is nothing like summer in New York, she thought to herself as she made her way briskly down 6th

Avenue to hail a cab to Brooklyn. It was June and the eyelids

of summer were just peeling open to rise and awaken. The

timid breeze blew occasionally on the well-traveled streets of

Manhattan, resurrecting the varying smells that lifted off of

them. The streets were an entity unto themselves. Singing and

humming with energy and stories. They sang the chorus of

the colorful gumbo of variety that was New York City. The

roasted peanuts on the corner. The hot dogs opposite to it.

All calling out to you to buy them. New York seemed to try

to sell you something everywhere you stepped. Whether it

was a dream, an opportunity, or a deal.

   This was a far cry from Los Angeles. She couldn't

believe that she had finally mustered up the courage to leave

that place. The real question was why had she stayed so long?

Meandering through the streets in the backseat of the fast

moving cab she couldn't stop her mind from thinking about Walter and the memories they shared here in the city. On her last day in Los Angeles, Phoenix took one final trip to the beach in Malibu and looked into the distance where she had once stayed with her ex-boyfriend Walter Deveroux. The man that she thought she would marry. The love of her life, and the one man who had ultimately left her shattered and in pain.

The house was a house of hell and she had wanted nothing more than to get out of it for years. Finally she was here in New York City. A free bird. A place where Walter told her that she should not come alone and that she would never make it without him. She was eighteen then and for the next 6 years she devoted her all to him in hopes that he would honor her and his promises and do the same.

Phoenix ran her hands through her shoulder length brown hair revealing the two quarter carat diamond studs in both ears. This was one of the last pieces of her jewelry from Walter that she had refused to give up. They were essentially the final vestiges of her past and all that she had left of it.

Her eyes glistened with melancholy as she recalled the day they met when she was just a 15-year-old girl beginning her modeling career in New York. He had approached her smiling disarmingly during a break at the IMTA modeling convention. His dark eyes, gentle and caring, as he asked her why she was standing off alone by herself. Phoenix shrugged her shoulders, not exactly sure. He appeared to be youthful, with slight grey flecks in his beard. His skin was smooth and dark like coal as he offered to take her for some ice cream.

The two sat chatting as he commented on her intelligence and maturity.

"You're not like these others girls," he said. "You're going to make it."

Phoenix covered her mouth in nervous laughter. There was something comforting about Walter. He was nice and disarming. He gave her more compliments and reassurance than her father ever did. She liked him.

"I would love to photograph you," he said studying her face intently.

"I believe that you have the potential to be a very successful model."

The two kept in touch over the summer. First through letters as Phoenix was finishing high school at the command of her mother. The second through the infrequent phone calls Phoenix snuck to Walter whenever she could steal away the time. They did this for three years.

His name was Walter Deveroux. He had been married before but he was now separated. His daughter Haley was 10 years younger than Phoenix herself. Phoenix sent him pictures at his request showing her growth. After little protest from her mother, as long as she agreed to finish school, Phoenix was off to be with her man and start her new life.

On her 18th birthday he flew her to New York. She had been accepted on an art scholarship to Parsons School of Design and instead of staying in the dorms with the other first time students she had opted to stay with Walter.

His loft in Harlem was overwhelming. Filled with original photos of Beverly Johnson, Pat Cleveland, and Janice

Dickinson. He was a master photographer that loved the human form. Women were everywhere displayed posed and postured throughout his home. The white walls holding up the background. Contemporary art pieces sat on the glass tables and shelves throughout the apartment. Red vases and porcelain elephants where neatly displayed in cases and on shelves. In the kitchen Walter showed his distinct propensity towards health with an unrelenting spread of fresh seasonal fruits on the countertops. This was different from her modest working class lifestyle in Michigan. Everything about his home and life just seemed so glamourous.

"So, what do you think?" he said looking at her eyes widening as she took everything in.

"This is amazing Walter."

Her smile betrayed her natural coolness. He walked over to her turning her shoulders to face him. He could feel her tremble beneath his fingertips her eyes staring up at him as he touched her.

"Do you know how long I have dreamed about this moment?"

She shook her head no.

"I dreamt of you coming here for a long time. I dreamt of you walking through those doors and more importantly I wanted to show you this."

He walked her over to the white partition in the far right corner of the room where his ornate bed lied. Above the four canopied bedposts was a picture of a glamorous and pensive looking Phoenix?

"I like to call this picture. Flight of the Phoenix," he said.

"When did you take this Walter?" she asked.

"I snapped you deep in thought when you weren't looking," he said. "That is when I walked over to you. You inspired me. You were such a beautiful vision that I couldn't help myself. I couldn't and didn't believe that a woman so perfect existed. At that moment I had to photograph you," he said walking behind her and rubbing her shoulders.

"I wanted to capture your innocence and your beauty on camera." Phoenix stood grounded in one place. Her spaghetti strapped Calvin Klein dress he bought her revealing the tautness of her breasts, which rose as he spoke. Walter walked over to his oak wood nightstand and took out his camera. The silence hung in the air as they looked at each other.

"You want to model don't you Mon Cherie." She nodded her head yes, not sure how to please him, yet wanting to.

"Then model."

She stared at him directly in his eyes as she walked past him and over to the white bed spread. She lifted herself up onto the bed never taking her eyes off of him, her bony knees hanging over the edge. Walter exhaled as he began to snap her photograph. Taking his cue she swung her hair around covering her eyes and began seducing him. She pretended that the camera was him. She felt herself getting tired after an hour of this game and laid her back on the bed, staring at the ceiling. Walter shouted for her to not stop and keep going but her young mind was running out of ideas. She stretched her legs out on the bed her dress above her knees revealing her white panties.

"I can't think of anything else to do," she said.

"Do that." He said moving in closer. "Do just what you are doing, being yourself."

He stepped in closer with his camera hoisting himself up on the bed and placing himself next to her snapping one final shot lowering his camera. His face was just inches from hers. He could feel the heat from her sweet breath as he stared into her brown eyes.

Phoenix's chest heaved. She reached her hand up and placed her index finger on his mouth; her chipping red nail polish playing with the insides of his cheeks. He took her finger to his lips and gently kissed them as she rose up off the bed and slowly moving in to kiss him. She kept her mouth closed against his in hesitation. His eagerness overtook him as he hungrily grabbed her face and savagely licked her neck, eventually finding his way back to her mouth.

She began to kiss him harder and deep until she heard him moan. He pulled her face away and looked at her. This woman child girl was attempting to take control of him.

"Wait," he said. I want to do this right. He carried her into the bathroom and placed her in the shower. He lathered up her body as she stood receiving his attention. He shaved every hair on her body and washed her hair. He carried her out of the shower, laying lithe body on the bed as he gingerly oiled her body from the tips of her feet and rested them at her temples. She laid back and closed her eyes as he rubbed every part of her. He treated her as if she were a newborn baby taking extra care not to break or hurt her.

"You okay." He said. "Yeah, I'm fine."

"You like the shower?" "Yeah, I did." "You okay?"

"Yeah, I'm fine." She laughed.

"Just relax," he said. He laid her naked back horizontally on the bed and looked at her. The light of the full moon over the city flowed through the windows of the loft.

"Let me take care of you," he said. He stared at her body her chest heaving up and down in anticipation. Her legs opened as he bent down to kiss her thighs. Her body trembled and stiffened slightly as he touched her. He parted her legs wider with his hands and kissed her inner thighs. He could feel the warmth of her flower on his forehead as he

16

went higher. Tiny whimpers seeped from her mouth as he moved higher between her legs, which were beginning to shake with excitement and fright. He tested the waters by gently flicking his tongue over the wetness that was coming out of her. She let out a small sigh as she gripped his shoulders. He flicked the area again feeling eager as he dove in licking and sucking and tasting her. Walter's shoulders heaved as he licked deep and in circles. He gripped her like a cowboy wrestling with a deer. Her tender body wriggled beneath his hands as he sucked her juices letting them float and simmer down his throat. Her body shook uncontrollably as he went in faster wanting all of her. She let out a loud scream before she cried. Unsure of what had just happened to her. He came up to her and held her in his arms.

"You okay?"

"Yes, I dreamed of this moment in my head as well. But, I had wanted to please you too." Walter looked at her and smiled. "Don't you worry about that precious, you please me enough." They hugged tightly as the fell asleep in each other's embrace.

Beep! Beep! Phoenix was startled by a loud sound of the cabdriver's horn.

"Move! Asshole you!" he said.

The cabdriver had almost made a near miss with a family of four in slightly banged up two door civic. Phoenix, feeling a little flustered from her daydream, tried to straighten up and peek at the meter. Feeling a bit anxious to hurry and arrive at her friend's house.

Tomorrow was going to be a special day. She was turning twenty-eight and already she felt so much more mature than she did last year.

As they approached the well-lit block filled with freshly painted and newly renovated brownstones the cab pulled over to the side.

"Yes, right here." She said reaching a delicate French manicured hand into her Balenciaga bag and handing him a twenty. "Keep the change."

Chapter Two

She walked down the street searching for the red brownstone with gold ballerina slippers hanging from the door. Laila had been on her way to becoming a principle dancer with the Alvin Ailey Company until she had a horrible knee accident that disrupted her brief career. Since then she had started her own event planning business, which was becoming very successful with the city's elite entertainment and sports crowd.

The two women hadn't seen each other since college and it had been a long overdue reunion.

"Oh my goodness! She finally made it," Laila squealed out the second floor window of her brownstone. "Wait right there I am coming down to get you."

The two women hugged and laughed excitedly as if no time had passed between them. "Hey, let me show you inside," Laila said grabbing her bag. "I restored the most of this place myself and I am so proud of it."

Laila looked radiant in the white wrap dress that fell just above her knees showing off the tan she acquired on one of her recent trips to Miami. Her golden highlights accentuated her natural glow and essence.

"You look beautiful as ever," Phoenix said.

"I'm just trying to keep up with you and all your diamonds," Laila said gesturing towards Phoenix's earrings. "Those earrings are life giving girl!"

The two friends laughed as Laila gave her the grand tour of her two story brownstone. Each room was beautifully decorated with cream and silver accents which she described as "to die for a thousand times."

"Would you like a glass of wine?" Laila asked pouring a glass of Sauvignon Blanc.

"Ah, you know I gave up drinking right? It affects my creativity."

"Actually, I didn't know that." She said placing the extra glass to the side. "Shame. You were always so much fun when you drank."

"More like a mess. I am attempting to try things the sober and enlightened route these days," Phoenix said with a wry smile.

Laila shot her a look. "On your birthday? In New York City? Honey that's way too boring. Drink up."

"Where are we going tonight?" Phoenix asked.

"We are going to one of the most exclusive events in the city tonight," Laila said her eyes widening with joy. Phoenix sat up in her seat on the couch. This was going to be good.

"This party is so exclusive," she said. "That I am not even throwing it. I have nothing to do with it. We are just invited. That's major in itself."

"Well, whose party is it?" Phoenix said.

Laila paused smiling, bubbling with anticipation.

"Are you ready?"

"Who is it? C'mon," Phoenix prodded.

Laila flung her golden locks over her shoulder and superficially studied her manicure, riding the suspense.

"Did I mention I only got two passes to this event?" she said looking up.

"I'm going to hurt you Laila James."

"Dexter. Stiles," Laila said as if she just dropped a bomb.

Phoenix crinkled her brows unimpressed.

"Who is Dexter Stiles?" she asked.

"Girl, you're kidding right? I know you been in France and Los Angeles and all but you don't know who *Dexter Stiles* is?" Laila said.

"Dexter Stiles is a major business man and music mogul in New York. He owns so much stuff that his net worth is unaccountable. He is only 30 something years old, and a notorious asshole but, he throws the best parties in the city. Anybody, who is *anybody*, will be there."

24

"So I take it we're the anybody's?"

"No, I'm the anybody. You're just my friend," Laila joked.

"And I did mention that you were a model, and the former protégé of Walter Deveroux. So that helped," she said.

The room fell silent at the mention of Walter's name.

"Are you ok Phe?" Laila asked.

Phoenix eyes widened as if she had seen a ghost. She tried to changer her expression but the mention of Walter's name had sent a chill up her spine.

"Is Walter going to be there?" Phoenix said.

"I don't think so. I just made it up. Why?"

Phoenix ran her slender fingers along her smooth black hair that had begun to lift off her shoulders at the mention of Walter's name.

"No reason. I just wasn't really prepared to see him that's all."

"I thought you were over that Phoenix? I thought that's why you came to New York after Paris to work and to forget all of that."

"I did. It's just still very difficult with everything that happened between us."

"You still never told me what those things were?" said Laila her eyes softening. She looked over at her friend whose small shoulders were quivering. It scared Laila to see her this way. Phoenix was normally the strong one and to see her revert back to a broken state worried her.

"Look Phe, he's not going to be there. Let's just get

ready and go have a good time."

She grabbed Phoenix by the shoulders playfully shaking her

to lighten the mood.

"Weren't you the one that was saying that you needed

some loving from a new man?"

"Yeah, I did say that."

"Weren't you the one saying that you wanted a new

experience?

"Yes, that was me, you got me."

'Well, c'mon let's go and have a good time. Hell, we

are going to Dexter Stiles' Halloween party." Laila jumped up

onto her cream couch bouncing around like a kid at the

thought of all the eligible young fly and flashy bachelors that were going to be there.

"Girl, it is on. Dexter is mine and I don't care if he got a girlfriend or not. It's over for that bitch. Especially once I pull out the red leopard Roberto Cavalli." She walked away towards the white-carpeted steps that led to her bedroom and threw a look over her shoulders. "Legs for days."

Phoenix laughed. Laila was still as sassy as ever. You would've thought that she was the famous model whose porcelain doll image had graced the pages of magazines and television shows.

Laila sashayed up the carpeted steps and into her bedroom. The fresh smell of perfume floated throughout the walls. She took off her green teal dress and threw it on the queen-sized bed. This bed was a statement in itself. It was enormous in stature with white sheer curtains that hung down covering the cream lace bedspread and its fluffy white pillows. Laila had entertained many a man in this bed. Lately she had hoped to share it with one man. She looked over at her cell phone, still no call from Jacob.

"I guess he has to take care of his *situation*," Laila sighed. Her eyes welled up with tears as she thought of Jacob and how she hadn't talked to him all week. She really had wanted to take him to the party and show him off to all of her friends and associates in the city, but his Friday nights seemed to be getting busier and busier. What was even crazier is that all the times Laila had invited him over and into her bed he had always refused to sleep with her. Enough of that

she thought. It was party time and she was not even going to

give Jacob any action.

Phoenix looked around Laila's apartment in

wonderment. Her taste was something that could have come

straight from the pages of Metropolitan Home. Phoenix was

proud of her friend, she had been doing well for herself it

seemed. Laila was the typical New York socialite. She had the

designer clothes, the renovated brownstone, and she had

started her own company. Phoenix wandered over to the

photos that were tacked on to the refrigerator. Many of them

showed Laila with a handsome chocolate brother. *He's fine*,

Phoenix thought. *I wonder if this is the infamous Jacob I am always*

hearing about.

Phoenix began reflect on the fact that she had moved back to New York and leaving her ostensibly fabulous life in Paris behind. She was so happy to see her friend again. Her life had begun to feel isolated and lonely in Los Angeles.

Laila reappeared in the living room with a red tiger print dress that showed off her stunning legs in the front and her toned back when she swirled around.

"Wow you look fabulous."

"Thank you, thank you," said Laila. "Now you need to go and get dressed so we can go."

Phoenix quickly went upstairs to change. Her mind began wandering on to Walter and the possibility of running into him.

"I can't believe Laila dropped his name at the door," she said emptying her make-up bag. "After all the things I went through with him, he's the last person I want to see."

Walter Deveroux, the modern day Henry Higgins who attempted to turn thread into gold with his Liza Doolittle Phoenix. Yet he was ill-equipped to fan the flames of her rising star. He became ferocious with his control. He controlled everything all the way down to the foods she ate, the clothes she wore and who became her friends. The unspeakable things he did to her caused her to flee. She knew in her heart that although she was broken everything around her was not.

Phoenix desperately wanted to get away from Walter's shadow and make a name for herself. Although she wanted these things a small part of her felt lost without Walter and she wondered if she could truly make it without him. He claimed to have made her and that she wouldn't stand a chance on her own.

Deep in her heart she felt that she could have soared so much farther had she had not been under the vice grip of his clutches.

She stood in the mirror applying her make-up. Carefully placing false lashes at the corners of her lids in order to accentuate her light brown almond shaped eyes. Despite Laila's silly joke, she was a little curious to see who would be at this party.

"This is good for the summer I think."
She said to herself as she spun around in the mirror looking at her legs. She placed her gold jeweled sandals that laced up her ankles on her feet, sprayed on her Chanel Mademoiselle

perfume and ran a brush over her hair. Her earrings sparkled as she reached into her bag for two additional items to complete the outfit. She pulled out a small sapphire ring with diamond clusters on the sides and a diamond encrusted bracelet, and walked downstairs.

"Fierce honey!" Laila screamed holding her second glass of wine in her hands and obviously feeling its affects.

"Thanks love," Phoenix said. "I think we are ready to do this. Dexter Stiles here we come."

Chapter Three

The moon shone like a diamond in the sky reminding the women that tonight was going to be a night to remember. The girls pulled up to The Lounge amazed at the line. There were over a hundred people standing in and around the velvet rope that separated the happy partiers from those desperately trying to gain entrance. Huge bodyguards dressed in all black ordered by Dexter Stiles stood guard at the entrances. This was not a pick and choose line this was an invite only affair. Only the rich, fabulous and well-connected were here to celebrate Dexter's birthday as well as his 15th year in the business. It had been a hard and arduous climb and Dexter was known to give back generously to his supporters.

The black suited men seemingly handled the massive crowd that was accumulating outside of the doors with ease.

Like well-trained secret service militia, they carefully screened each person that tried to bribe, con and finagle their way into the party. Some people that were turned away were some of Hollywood's well- known actors, models and directors. Dexter wasn't into to names. He was only into the best. He only wanted the best and the brightest around him and the even brighter at his party. He was not interested in the hangers on; he was interested in those he felt could make his empire great.

The solid gold doors of The Lounge were illuminated by the two spotlights that were waving from the sidelines of the red carpet. Everybody who was anybody was attending this party tonight. It was the hottest ticket in town.

"Man you know who I am. Listen to me, I know Dexter. We used to work together ok? Trust me. I should be in here," said a young attractive man with a serious will to get in.

"I already told you Shawn man, if you don't have an invite, you have to leave. I know who you are, but Dexter asked me to specifically follow the list and your name is not on it," the bouncer said unflinchingly.

"Look, me and Dexter were supposed to have a meeting tonight and he knew about it. He knows I'm supposed to be in that party tonight."

He reached into the side pocket of his cream linen coat and produced a wad of cash. "Can I persuade you one time? There won't be any problems."

"Sorry Sean. I love you brother, but this party is not for you."

The man, thoroughly disgruntled, walked aggressively past the girls and muttering under his breath.

"Tell Dexter this is not over!" he yelled backing away from the club.

The girls gave him a sideward glance as they made their way to the front. Laila paused reaching into her black clutch to grab her silver cigarette case. She pulled out a smoke and lit it up with her diamond encrusted lighter. She squinted and inhaled as she put the case back into her purse as they made their way to the front.

"Now, I'm ready," she said taking a puff. "Let's do this."

The girls made their way to the front pushing past the desperate faces of onlookers that were not being swayed to leave although repeatedly asked. Laila walked over to the burly Puerto Rican bouncer whose cold eyes matched his motionless stance behind the rope.

"Hi we're on Tonya's list, my name is Laila James."

He paused for a moment from looking at his list to take a double take at Phoenix who was looking around at all the action.

"What's up sexy? Like that dress," he said waving the girls in.

"Hey LaLa what's up!" said Steve the handsome six foot promoter from Stiles Management. He bounded over to Laila giving her a hug and kiss. He had done a lot of work for Tonya and recognized Laila immediately. "Hey girl, it's about time you got here. Let me take you to the VIP and we can get some drinks."

"That's what I'm talking about," Laila said. The girls grooved and danced through the crowd as they held onto Steve towards VIP. The area here was much milder than the main floor that was filled with go go dancers, women that were scantily clad, men in fish tanks, and life sized blow up dolls. The Lounge was anything but that. It was a two level powerhouse club that was one of the biggest in the city with its red interior and stone walls that were reminiscent of a cave. A waterfall dripped cool water down the back wall from the 2nd to the first floor. The backdrop of the white bar was lit up by blue florescent lights that gave the bar a feeling of floating on water.

Steve sat the women down on a red crushed velvet bed behind a white sheer sheet as he caught up with Laila. The waitress brought over a fresh bottle of champagne as they lounged back and listened to the thunderous spins of DJ Turnskillz.

The VIP had a house music vibe that was even sexier.

"Here you go cutie," Steve said handing a glass of bubbly to Phoenix.

"Happy birthday to me," she said taking a delicate swig. "Yeah, that's the way. You're a little star, I seen your pics and your flicks," Steve said. "You were on that show All for One, you played the daughter right?"

Phoenix nodded giggling. Phoenix nodded giggling. The bubbles of the champagne made her warm and fuzzy. Laila tapped her arm. "Hey, I heard Dexter just got here and he came in with his fiancé."

"Who?"

She is not all that," Laila said slurring her words. "She's just tall and skinny that's all. I think she's a supermodel though. I heard they're in another part of the club though. It's real private. We *have* to try and get up there."

Phoenix nodded at Laila as she went on and on about Dexter. She felt the need to move around and stepped from behind the white curtain and stood against the banister overlooking the main floor of the club. She watched the show that was going on beneath her.

She closed her eyes and let the music resonate through her body. She swallowed the last of her champagne and swayed her hips to the music. She began to dance seductively to no one in particular as she lost herself in the beat of the music. She jumped as she felt someone press up against her with their hands on her hips.

"Excuse, I don't want to dance," she said.

"What are you talking about? This is party," he said.

"So, you want to dance with me, you ask me nicely." she said.

"Okay, how much?" he said waving 300 dollars at her.

"Excuse me?"

"You heard me, how much to make you dance?"

"I'm not for sale?"

"Says who?"

"Says me. Besides you don't have what it takes to pay the price," she said.

The man laughed to himself. This was a feisty one, he thought.

"I know I could buy you better earrings than the ones you got on now," he said coyly.

She looked angrily into his beady black eyes that were taunting her. His dark thick eyebrows made him look menacing, yet attractive, as he stood formidably in his black suit.

"Why don't you save your money and put them towards some manners," Phoenix rolled her eyes.

"Look, I didn't mean to disrespect you," he said. "I looked down from my room upstairs and I noticed you dancing and having a good time and wanted to know if you would join me upstairs. There's some food up there if you're hungry."

She eyed him skeptically wondering how this man had an in on the upstairs room. Although she didn't want the company of anyone that night she was a little hungry.

"I'll go with you, on one condition," she said.

"What's that?" he said.

"Don't touch me again without permission."

"Hands to myself. I promise," he said placing his hands behind his back.

He smiled at her as they walked through a side entrance onto an elevator.

"Hi you doing sir?" the doorman said as he let the pair through.

"Cool, don't let anyone one else up okay Rick."

"Sure thing," Rick said.

Phoenix looked at him. He was attractive in a stern sort of way. His relaxed smile betrayed his eyes, which seemed hard and focused. They only seemed to soften slightly when he laughed.

"Don't let anyone else up, huh? What are you trying to do to me up here?" she said.

"Relax, you're safe," his face growing serious to emphasize his point. "See, there are other people up here. I just didn't want anyone else up here because I wanted to get a little work done. I don't want it crowded you know?"

"Work at a party?' she said.

"I'm always working baby. A man that is not working is not a good man. He's a man with no plan. Remember that."

The doors opened as he led her to a door at the end of the hall. The doors opened to a small Zen styled room. A few women parlayed on the black couch as slow jams came from the walls.

"Make yourself comfortable," he said pointing her to a lounge chair in the corner. "See, plenty of people. Enough people for you?" he said smiling.

"I guess so," she said.

"Would you like a drink?" he asked.

"What are you having?" she said.

"Water, that's all I mainly drink."

"Me too, well I had a glass of champagne in celebration of my birthday."

"When is your birthday?"

"Tomorrow."

"Interesting. I'll make us a special drink to toast since it's my birthday too. We're just connecting on all levels. First water and now our birthdays. It's beautiful actually." His cell phone rang as he walked over to the kitchen.

"Excuse me for a minute while I take this." Phoenix looked around the room. She recognized a few of the women scattered in various places throughout the suite. One of them was Nina Velez Cruz, a famous supermodel. The other was Hijoya Min, a Japanese actress from a lot of the urban flicks that were hot right now. The black girl cuddled up with the guy who looked like the owner of Marcus Mack the owner of Get Money records was none other than the award-winning actress Jennifer Harper. Who was this man? Phoenix wondered.

"Here's your drink," Dexter said smiling and handing her a reddish liquid.

"What is it," she asked.

"Cranberry juice and sprite. Our favorite," he smiled. "Let's go to the back room where there's a balcony and toast."

Phoenix followed him down the white carpeted hallway to a back master bedroom that had a balcony.

They stood out over the balcony and looked out onto the city. The city was beautiful and illuminated. It was gorgeous, more than she ever expected to experience on her birthday.

He studied her carefully as her eyes widened looking over the city. He stopped as she raised the glass to her lips.

"Wait, happy birthday?" he said toasting her cup. "I happen to know that people born on this day are very special people."

Phoenix smiled taken in by the night. Her mind went back to Walter. He was always good for surprising her like this.

"Your eyes are in another place right now. What are you thinking about?" he asked.

"Nothing really. Just a time, a long time ago."

They both stared into the night letting the breeze over take them. She began to shiver slightly as the wind blew. He took off his coat and handed it to her.

"Here, take my coat."

"Thanks," she said

"See, I'm not such a bad guy."

Phoenix wasn't sold. She had been in this situation plenty of times.

"You know when I was a little boy; I used to dream of one day owning the city. Not literally, but I wanted to make a lot of money and change my circumstances, for me, and my family," he said looking up at the sky.

"I was just a little knotty head kid 1st generation West Indian kid from Brooklyn. My father passed away when I was 13 and my mother took it hard. My brother and I had to work for her basically. We were so poor. One time I could hear my mother crying herself to sleep because she was so hungry. Me and my brother would just dream of getting rich and making it so she didn't have to cry anymore. Now I'm 30 years old and I did that times 10."

"That's amazing," Phoenix said. "Did you have to do anything illegal?"

"Actually I never did. I didn't want to bring shame to my father's name so we started different businesses. Selling things and saving money and my mom finally got a better job and I went to college. I don't advertise it because I have a year left to get my business degree but it would be nice. I like to finish what I start."

"I have an Associate's degree in Fashion Merchandising. Not quite what I wanted. I wanted to be a designer. I also wanted to model and act. But I went that direction or it chose me in a way."

He paused for a moment before he started laughing.

"You're a little short for high fashion but you're not bad to look at. I can see why you wanted to model. What do you do now?"

"The same thing. Trying to live my dreams I guess."

"How is your financial situation?"

"It's um, I, well-"

"Basically you're broke."

"I wouldn't go that far. I'm not where I want to be put it that way."

"Wow, that must be painful for you," he smirked. Phoenix had begun to feel warmed up to him. He had almost looked teary eyed as he reminisced about his life. Feeling uncomfortable he went back to the aggressiveness he had displayed when he met her downstairs.

"Don't move sweetheart," he said putting his cellphone to his ear and taking a call.

"This is Dexter," he said into the phone his face growing serious.

He kept his eye on her as he listened to the call and mouthed,

"So what's up?"

Phoenix looked quizzically at him wondering when the change had occurred.

"Tell Kirk I'm looking at the apartment on 5th Avenue for 11.5 million. And tell him to call TJ in the morning and settle it if it's good." His eyes were steely as he turned back to Phoenix.

"Sorry about that. So what's up? What's your name?" he said.

"My name is Kim and I think I better get going, my friend is probably looking for me," Phoenix said heading towards the door.

He grabbed her arm to stop her. She looked at his hands.

"No, I'm sorry, look you getting it all wrong."

"No, I have to go really. I have an appointment early in the morning so I need to get some sleep."

Phoenix placed her glass on the ledge and started for the door.

"It's been real, thanks for the juice."

"Can, I call you?" he said as she walked away.

"I can't. I don't have a number. See you around."

Phoenix walked past the scene in the living room to the elevator. She just wanted to get out. She didn't know who this man was but she didn't like the change that had come over

him and she just wanted to get back to Laila.

He came running out as she was boarding the elevator.

"Look, can I contact you and make sure you got

home safely?"

"I told you, I don't have a phone."

His eyes looked confused as she waved good-bye.

"Well nice meeting you Kim. Get home safe."

Phoenix felt like she may have left a bit too abruptly by the

look in the man's eyes as she left him. No matter, she

thought. He's just some guy who thinks that he can flash

some green and get the girls jumping. Look at him, he even

asked my name late.

She walked off the elevator and ran into Laila who was

dancing seductively with Steve. The crowd had begun to thin

out but the diehards kept it going.

Phoenix tapped her on the shoulder in attempts to break up

her dance fest.

"Phe, what's up girl? Where have you been?"

"I was upstairs in some private VIP room."

"With who?"

"Some guy, nothing special."

"So what's up? What are you doing down here, if you

were up there with a piece?"

"Long story La. I am going to catch a cab back to my

hotel. I got a message about a meeting tomorrow, so I need

to get some sleep."

"Okay, call me tomorrow so we can have lunch or something."

Phoenix stepped out into the cool New York night the streets in front of the club less agitated as she hailed a cab to the Soho Grand.

Chapter Four

It was nearly four in the morning and the party was finally winding down. All of his guests had left for the evening many hours before. While other people allowed their guests to stay all night he had a strict no lounging rule unless it had been previously discussed. Even then he liked to keep to himself. Dexter wasn't too big on company. The thought of people constantly hanging around all the time was unappealing to him. He knew other successful men that liked to keep entourages around them but he was not one of them. He liked to socialize but his home was his sanctuary and when it was time to retire everyone had to go.

Dexter sat behind his desk and called up his assistant Kiera. She was normally pretty good about the phone. He needed to know his meeting line up for tomorrow. The call went to voicemail but he noticed an email coming in and smiled. She sent him his calendar. Kiera was always on it without him even asking. She could just read his mind. Now if he could just get his own woman to be that attentive he would be set.

He tried to focus on the meetings he had to take care of that next morning, but his mind kept wandering back to Kim and what he said to her to make her leave so abruptly like that. Maybe I shouldn't have answered the phone in front of her he thought. Women hate that. He licked his lips. She was so sexy and gorgeous. There was something about her that was different and made him want to know her a little more. He was puzzled that she didn't leave her information. He didn't want to seem cocky but most of the women he ran across would have quickly left their number and dropped everything to stay and be with him.

"Kim from Paris huh?" he said. "I may have to put my bloodhounds on that situation."
He heard a knock at the door as a tall delicate beauty slinked in over to him and kissed his lips seductively.

"Why couldn't I get past your goons an hour ago to see you baby?" she said.

"I didn't want anyone up here," he said.

"Why? Who was up here D? I saw you lead a girl up through the club."

"Don't start Lisa, it's my birthday," he said.

"I am not trying to argue," she said her eyed softening sensing his coldness.

"I just wanted to know if you were coming home to night or staying here. I didn't want to be waiting for you if you weren't coming."

Her brown eyes bore into him looking for answers. He looked at the innocence that emanated from her eyes as they pleaded to him for answers. He didn't assuage her as he looked back and forth between her face and his phone. She propped every inch of her long lean 5 foot 9 caramel legs on his desk and crossed them. Her blue lace dress started riding high on her thighs and she pouted. Dexter fought his natural reaction to grab her and throw her on the desk and screw her brains out and send her home. Those were the main emotions that she inspired in him. Everything with him and her was so animalistic and primal it was hard to have a real relationship with someone that you either wanted to choke, cry or screw them senseless.

Lisa was his fiancée. He never considered himself to be possessive until her met her. Not only was she beautiful she was a former Ms. Atlanta. But she was a bit young. He had given her a 5-carat ring just to shut her up and to keep her close. She wasn't the brightest woman ever, and she could be clingy, but she knew how to make a man feel like a man. Plus the sex was good and he didn't want that to stop.

She tossed her shoulder length jet black ringlets across her back hoping to woo him off of the phone. He rubbed her thighs as she flirted. Take your panties off he mouthed. She smiled and without blinking used her ab muscles to lift her legs in the air to remove her panties exposing a perfectly waxed mound.

Dexter placed his hand on her chest and began to lick and kiss her deeply. He tried to go slowly but soon he picked her up and was carrying her around on his face. "Yes daddy ugh! Oh Dex!" she screamed grabbing his head. He walked them around from his desk and tossed her into the air onto the couch. He was going to hurt her tonight.

"Oh no what?" Lisa said her eyes widened. She always got a little nervous when Dexter got that crazed look in his eyes.

"You know what time it is? Turn around on the couch."

Lisa did as she was told as she felt his hands lifting dress up from the back. She felt herself getting wet as he rubbed his hands over her behind before entering her with his fingers. He was so rough that she moaned loudly.

She knew better than to tell him to stop or that it hurt or it may really hurt. But she knew what was coming.

WHACK!

"Ouch!" she cried. "No please. No not that." she said. "I don't like that game."

WHACK WHACK!

"Yes," he said. "This is the game we are going to do. This is for you questioning me. I told you about that. Now apologize."

WHACK WHACK. WHACK.

He let his hand come roughly down on her behind 10 ten times before entering her.

"No, No…Yes. Yes," she cried.

"I thought you were saying no," Dexter said thrusting to climax. The two trembled together. Dexter looked at Lisa who was looking flushed in the faced and kissed her deeply. He remembered at that moment why he wanted to marry her. She was a perfect fit.

There was just no questioning her beauty and her fierce loyalty. She was West Indian like him but she hailed from the suburbs of Buckhead, GA and came from a prominent family of doctors. Her family had done well for themselves and equally was well for their daughter. Lisa herself was a Spelman Alumnus. Dexter at one time questioned why she would want him if not for his money.

Early in his life he wouldn't have been able to get a woman like Lisa unless he was rich or came from a prominent black family. But he was from the streets of

Bedstuy, Brooklyn. Every day on his way to school he had to avoid the drug dealers, addicts and the O.G.'s that hung on the stoops of brownstones daily just so he could get an education.

He was obsessed with making money. He wanted out of Bedstuy and into a better brownstone where he could buy the hottest fashions and go the finest places he walked by in Manhattan and live the life he always dreamed of. He never just wanted an arm piece woman. He wanted a partner. Yet he couldn't resist the beauty of Lisa Whitaker when he saw her. She had the appearance of a diamond or a cultured pearl. She was a novelty. Something that only came around once in a lifetime and he got her.

Dexter questioned if she would be able to be a solid mother for his children and help him to build a legacy. She was young and immature. When they met at the boxing

match in Vegas two years ago she was only 21. She slinked

over to him in a revealing yellow dress as she sat with some

of her girlfriends. They were partying and dancing and having

a ball at their table. Dexter had been watching her for a while

as she interacted with her friends. He tried to stay low key at

his table as his eye kept meeting that of the beautiful Lisa

Whitaker.

      "What are you drinking?" he asked.

      "Moet?" she said.

She sipped her champagne slowly letting a little spill onto her

chin that Dexter immediately wiped off with his hand.

      "What's your name?" he said

      "Lisa."

      "I know yours," she said giggling. "Dexter Stiles."

"Almost," he said. "My full name is Dexter Quran Stiles. Most people don't know that. But I wanted you to know."

"Thanks, I feel special," she smiled." They both laughed and sat looking in each other's eyes for a while before Dexter spoke.

"There's some real unfortunate stuff that's going down with my company at the moment. I may lose it. Would you still be with me?"

She thought about it before taking another sip of her champagne.

"No," her brown lids lowering over her honey colored-eyes. She meant it.

When he went to pay for the tab Lisa grabbed the bill from the waitress' hand. "I got this one since your company is on its last leg and all."

He sat in fascination. There was never a woman that had done anything like that. Most women were content with sitting back and allowing him to pay for everything. He was the human ATM, and they the tax write offs. She quickly signed the bill and raised her glass to Dexter.

"Thanks for the convo," she said. She stood up and spun off on her heels and started dancing with her girlfriends, oblivious to Dexter and his entourage. He liked how she played hard to get. He sat back and watched as the different ball players and businessmen whispered in her ear. She was eating it up. She was used to the attention.

On her way out he stopped her and asked her for her number and where she was staying. She said at the Venetian. The next morning her had 12 dozen roses in all different colors delivered to her room. She was very surprised and said that she had to fly to Zimbabwe the next day but she would call as she soon as she got back and she did. The night she stepped foot on dry land he sent for her and romanced her and she never left his apartment on the upper west side. That was when she was truly beautiful. That was when she was strong. Lately she had seemed to be falling apart and he was growing tired of her. She wasn't adding to the equation.

She walked away reluctantly to the other room. As Dexter called around to try and find Kim from Paris. He had her face emblazoned on his mind. He was going to find her.

Chapter Five

The morning sky was cool and gray as it hung over the New York skyline. The sound of cars on the avenue below bustled with people scurrying to get to work. Men in gray and black suits hurried across the crosswalk like scattering ants as the wind blew their ties under their chins. Stone faced women stared singularly focused towards their destination as they warded off incessant pieces of paper promising free gifts thrust toward their hands. Dark pantsuits and summer shoes in a sea of pulled back ponytails and buns gripped their coffees and their summer clutches as they maneuvered through the crowds towards the imposing office buildings. The fresh smell of coffee and bagels rose in the air from the coffee truck as people rushed to get their coffee. Phoenix watched all of the action from the balcony of her suite. She decided to order room service. She ordered a chai tea latte with soy and croissant with jam. A soft boiled egg with a fresh bowl of strawberries a small chocolate, her indulgence.

She didn't want to have anything too heavy for breakfast since she was going in for a meeting at DQS Advertising for their new perfume and cosmetic line. This was her first meeting in New York in a long time. The market was new to her all over again and now that she didn't have the wing of Walter to hide under she knew that she would have to do everything herself. She picked out the yolk of her egg and ate its soft white shell. She flipped through the stack of magazines that were on the table looking at the different clothing ads. DQS was a becoming a major powerhouse in the industry. She hadn't heard of them in Los Angeles too much, but now she was seeing the ads starring Lisa Whitaker, the former Miss USA, actress and model, in most of their campaigns. "Wow she's gorgeous," Phoenix said to herself picking at her strawberries. "Why would they want to get rid of her for a new model?"

She shook the thoughts out of her head as she sipped the last bits of her tea. Her doe eyes looked courageously out to the terrace and onto the city. Now was not the time to have doubts or question her purpose and why she was doing this. She was beginning to need this job. She wasn't going to be able to live like this forever not if she was smart. Yet like Walter always told her, you have to fake it until you make it and that's exactly what she was trying to do.

That's what everyone in the party seemed to be doing, faking it.

Phoenix thought of the crowd of dancers that flooded the floors of the club that night and the mysterious gentlemen that called had brought her to the secret upper room. He was charming although he had turned back to the way that she thought he would almost instantly. New York was definitely going to be a city to be reckoned with. It's fast talk, with even faster intentions. But as they say, if you can make it here you can make it anywhere, and Phoenix was determined to make it here. Although she tried hard not to think about it, the man that she met the previous night kept popping in her mind.

She quickly showered and dressed and called a car service to pick her up and take her to midtown. She chose to wear a fitted yellow Gucci tank that made her skin look like the sunshine. She pulled her hair away from face in a low chignon to draw accentuate her facial features. She didn't want anything to distract from her face, which is what the campaign was really looking for. She slipped on a classic black jumpsuit and some stilettos and headed out the door. She looked back at the door of her hotel room. "Hopefully, I won't have to see you anymore room. Wish me luck."

"So where were you last night?" Laila asked Jacob who sat on her couch unaffectedly.

"I told you, I was working really late, I fell asleep at the office and I didn't make it out in time to meet you"

"So what? The next day when you woke up and realized that you had forgotten our date why didn't you call or say anything explaining yourself?"

Jacob shifted uncomfortably on Laila's couch. He was getting a little aggravated with her line of questioning. The fact that he forgot should have been enough for her but as usual it wasn't. He tugged at his ear and looked sheepishly up at her green eyed glaring gaze. Frustrated she turned from him, grabbing her coffee and sitting in a chair on the other side of the room. There was actually no excuse for him not coming by except that he couldn't make it out of his house.

Things didn't go as planned and he didn't have the place to himself like he had hoped. He watched Laila as she sat in the love seat facing the window overlooking the sidewalk. Her hair stiffened in wet strands over her shoulders as she looked out at the passersby. The two sat in silence.

Laila watched as two brown birds danced and playfully chased each other in the streets playing love games. She looked over her shoulder at Jacob who had his head in his hands. *Too much of a coward to tell the truth*, she thought.

She knew that he had been in an on again off again relationship for the last eight years but that shouldn't stop him from opening up to her and telling her the truth about whatever this situation was. A knot formed in Laila's stomach as she sipped her coffee and returned to looking out of the window pulling the collars of her red silk robe closer to her body.

Jacob let out a cough in order to loosen the atmosphere a little. Laila gave no notice as she methodically brought the coffee cup to her lips and took small sips. She reached into her robe pocket and lit a clove. Jacob knew that she was smoking in order to hurt him. She knew that he detested smoke, but obviously she had reached the point of wanting to disrespect him. She had reached the point of wanting to hurt him. He started to say something to her but his heart fell as he saw a tear roll down her cheek. He had never seen her cry before. The Laila James he knew was the tough imposing Brooklyn bad girl who drank her Courvoisier straight up with a splash of pineapple. The Laila James he knew had men falling at her stilettos as she balanced them all like desserts on her tray. Not the puttering princess who needed him to kiss her knee when she fell off her bike.

"Do you want me to go?" he said.

Laila sighed. Her shoulders hunched forward as she dropped the remains of her cigarette in her coffee and placed her head on the back of her couch. She said nothing.

Jacob stood and smoothed out his blue DQS tracksuit and grabbed his keys. Laila didn't make a move.

The cunning boyish look that was usually fixated on Jacob's face was replaced by fear.

"Laila, talk to me. Do you just want me to leave?"

She remained frozen on the sofa; her body heaving slowly up and down. Jacob walked over to her body which for the first time looked small and fragile to him and sat down next to her. It was so quiet it stung. He could hear her shallow breathing as small moans leaked out. His hand trembled as he rubbed her hair.

He was afraid to lift her face unsure of what would be under there. He pulled the damp strands of her blond hair back as he kissed her ear. He could feel the heat rising from skin that was being shielded from him underneath her arm. He kissed her cheek, as he slowly pulled her face, which was offering a slight resistance out from under her arms. Her face looked up at him, stained with tears.

Her face expressionless and lifeless. Her eyes puffy and pink. She looked at him with the most defeated look Jacob had ever seen. He pulled her over to him and hugged her.

"I'm sorry Laila." He said lifting her robe and rubbing the smooth skin on her back. "I really am, please don't be mad at me."

She laid her head on his shoulders as he rubbed her back. He meant it. Seeing her like this he felt helpless. His

81

brother Quincy warned him not to get involved with anyone, but he was so smitten by this woman that he couldn't deny himself. She made him laugh when she wasn't angry. She was definitely fun. There were just extenuating circumstances that could not be helped at this time. She pulled away from him looking him in his eyes.

"Don't do that to me again Jacob. This is the third time this month that you've broken plans with me."

The taxi pulled up in front of the Broadway offices of

DQS Enterprises as she went in through the glass doors she

was impressed by the impressive aesthetic. The black granite

walls looked to be hand carved. The steel metal elevator

doors that were on opposite sides of the guard desk, made for

an equally opposing visual of strength.

"How can I help you miss?" the old gentleman at the

security desk asked. He was an old black man. He had the

gentle ease of a man that perhaps didn't need this job as if

here were someone's uncle and had been given a favor.

"I am here for Janet Taylor of DQS Marketing."

The old security took his time looking slowly form her face to

the computer screen.

"Can I see your picture identification young lady?"

Phoenix reached into her tan leather bag and pulled out her ID. The man grabbed it and studied it with a sly smile.

"You old. Here I thought you were a little young something."

Phoenix winked and gave her best smile although she was not amused at his comment.

"I'm kind of in a hurry. I don't want to be late."

"Sure thing pretty. Don't mean to move slow."

Phoenix was growing impatient as the man slowly transferred information into the system and asked her if she was familiar with the Ojay's tune that was playing on the overheard.

"No I don't," she said curtly. "Before my time."

"We'll you got to make sure that you keep yourself educated on all aspects of life. The old school and the new school," he said handing her the pass.

"I will keep that in mind." Phoenix snatched the pass and raced to the elevator. The receptionist in the office of DQS led her into the conference room. It was an empty and sterile feeling meeting room. In the room was one long table with six chairs flanking each side and a grand leather chair at the head.

Phoenix sat there for ten minutes drinking her Pellegrino wondering when the meeting was going to actually get started. She was grew imminently restless and was about to stand to go when a man in a sleek black Armani suit and crisp white sans tie came bounding in and apologizing for running behind.

"Are you Miss Mitchell?" he said extending his hand to Phoenix.

"Yes."

"I'm Dexter Stiles." He said as they shook hands. The two paused.

"You were at my party last night right? Kim?" Phoenix feeling the shame of her small lie, smiled weakly, as she let go of his hand.

"Have a seat," he said eyeing her with suspicion. "I saw your photos awhile back in a very small and obscure French magazine. I don't remember the name but it caught my eye. You're a little short for high fashion and skinny for average girl standards but you have some weight on you." Phoenix discreetly rubbed her hips. Weight? What weight?

Dexter rambled on as an assistant set up his presentation and he glanced through her book.

"You haven't really done much, but I liked your look. It has a nostalgic quality for me. That's why I called you in." He leaned back in his chair staring at her with his eyes squinted. "Life got a funny way huh?"

"What do you mean sir?" Phoenix said.

"You know life got a funny way of putting people in their place.'

"Right," She said. "So what in particular did you think of when you saw my photos?"

"Slow down. I'm running this meeting. Let's take a look at this presentation here on the screen."

Phoenix sat up straight at the tone of his voice.

"I read your resume. You got a few credits did some spreads nothing major," he shrugged. "In the past we've been fortunate to work with some top models and actresses for the brand. Elizabeth Monet she was the launch of our first campaign. She was a true professional and veteran. She had a racially ambiguous look and that worked well for us. She was a great girl." He pointed to Lisa's picture on the wall. "We also had Lisa Whitaker the former Miss USA. She is our current model on the fashion side. She has a lot of universal appeal. For us, that really made a strong statement in terms of the luxury and value of the brand that we were trying to convey. These women have some major accomplishments and they fit into the larger message of the company that we are trying to establish globally. Both of those women had an unattainable beauty that the public identified with as an

aspirational goal."

Phoenix shrunk in her seat. Dexter went on.

"With DQS Style we always wanted to give off an air

of exclusivity that was desirable. You want to be a part of

DQS which basically is the pinnacle of the American dream,"

he said clicking through the last slides of the presentation.

Phoenix felt her nervousness rising in her shoulders

with every picture of a beautiful and accomplished woman he

scrolled through. She reached for her Pellegrino but ended

up knocking it over onto the table.

"I'm sorry," she said looking around for napkins.

"No sweat" he said. He said. "It's just a six thousand

dollar table."

"Right," she said.

"The napkins are behind you," he said.

He watched her from behind as she hurriedly grabbed paper towels to wipe up the water. She looked nervous and Dexter found it funny. He liked to make women jump. The room was thick and silent as he watched her carefully wipe the spill. She sat down swatting her bangs from her eyes. Her gentle face showing signs of agitation.

"You look very pretty cleaning."

"Excuse me Mr. Stiles?"

"You didn't have to wipe that up you know. I have people that do that. I just said the napkins were behind you. I was just making you aware. You chose to clean and I like a woman that looks good cleaning that's all."

Phoenix began to gather her things.

"Well, I guess I would be better served in someone's kitchen and not on the pages of your campaign," she scoffed.

"Hey, you need to lighten up. This is a six-figure deal on the table. Are you going to let a little joke take you out the running for some real cash flow in your life? Fame?" he said, eyes twinkling with starry excitement.

"You go to squash your dreams so quick because of your pride?"

Phoenix sat back down in the chair. She did need this money and more importantly she needed this campaign to prove to herself that she could make it without Walter.

"Your right," she said swirling in her chair to face him head on. "Perhaps I should lighten up. So did you make all the ladies display their cleaning abilities before they got the campaign or is that something you saved for me?"

"Look, I know your history Ms. Mitchell or should I say Kim right? I know your man, that weasel Walter Deveroux was on his way out. He wasn't focused anymore. Maybe you took his focus away because he used to be great. You stayed with him and were going nowhere. Now you need a job right?" Phoenix's bit her tongue. If she was so average and desperate why did he even want her to represent his aspirational brand?

"Look Dexter you just threw my pitiful life back at me right? You should know better than anyone that this is not easy, starting from the bottom. If I am so average and so desperate, why would you want to tarnish your brand with a nobody like me? Listen, you want me for this campaign?

Then send a contract over to my manager and I'll think about it."

Phoenix grabbed her bag and began storming out of the room when he ran over to the door and blocked her. He met her face eye to eye. He was so close she could feel his breath. "I need to leave," she said softer than she wanted to.

"Why did you tell me your name was Kim when it wasn't?" he said. His eyes peered through to her soul. "I thought I recognized you from your picture. I never forget a face."

"I didn't give you my number because you were not nice," she said.

Dexter moved his body closer and Phoenix bit her lip. She felt her knees growing weak with wishing he would

take her in his arms. She was angry at her body for
responding the way that it did. She turned slightly trying to
look away.

"Oh, I am an asshole? Is that what you want to say?
You know my life story? You just going to write me off like
that?" His breathe streaming steady from his nose was warm
against her face. Phoenix felt her stomach jump; a feeling of
anxiety and disgust.
"Out of my way," she whispered her arm pushing his arm
from in front of the door. Dexter was not to be denied.

"Have dinner with me," he said, words tumbling over
and out of his mouth as if trying to escape. "We can talk
about the campaign seriously. I have a meeting with some
people from Flashy magazine and I want you to come. I'll
pick you up at 9:00. We're going over to Mr. Chows."

Her shoulders fell. She looked into Dexter's eyes, which screamed sincerity. If dinner would be all it took to land her the DQS campaign she was willing to do it.

"Fine. I'll go with you to Mr. Chow's," she said moving closer into him attempting to regain her control. "But send a separate car for me. I don't want you getting the wrong idea."

"Anything you want Ms. Mitchell. I'll send a car for you."

"I'm at the Soho Grand," she said walking out the door.

"I know," he said. "I got you."

Phoenix walked out of the office with heart beating hard against her chest. As she made her way to the elevator of DQS a smile broke over her face. She put her hand to her face as she replayed Dexter's breath on her cheek. She closed

95

her eyes and imagined hips lips on her neck and his hands

roaming her body.

"Oh my God Phoenix, stay focused," she said

pressing the button on the elevator. As she clutched her

purse to her chest she couldn't help but wonder who was this

Dexter Stiles and why was he acting this way towards her.

Phoenix was unsure of how to take him. She didn't want to

be in his company but she was definitely up to going to Mr.

Chow's and weighing her options and opportunities.

Dexter's car arrived promptly at 9pm to pick up

Phoenix from her hotel room. She flounced down to the

lobby in a sexy white tunic dress and gold heels. Her bronzer was working wonders on her skin tone and she felt a small wave of nervousness at meeting Dexter for dinner. He was sexy and attractive but according to Laila he had definitely made his way through the women. Phoenix was going to make sure that she was not one of them. With her faux Chanel clutch in hand she tossed her hair over her shoulders and marched towards the long black car that awaited her. The driver, dapper in a black suit and bow tie, greeted her with a smile as she hopped in the car. She tried to ignore the sound of her rumbling stomach as she slide over the cool leather of the black seat.

"I could get used to this," she said surveying her surroundings. There had never been a time when she had been picked up by a car service. Walter would get picked up and taken around town for events when he was still on top producing indie films and shooting top models. Phoenix grew bitter at the thought. Walter always gave her an excuse about why her presence was not going to be needed alongside of him. Often she spent her nights a caged bird, staring into the ocean, her mind wondering where he might have been.

It was then that she decided to get busy and show Walter that she was just as worthy as the models he photographed and so she secretly took acting lessons on her own. At least if he was no longer impressed with her behind the camera he would be impressed with her in front on the camera. Those were the days of long nights and hard work as she ventured in secret to the city at night.

Feeling alive with her secret, and her new sense of self, she diligently honed her skills at the Stella Adler studio. It was her goal to become the best actress that she possibly could. She wanted this from deep inside of her. But she also wanted to please Walter. Yet when Walter's jobs became few and far between because of his mismanagement of funds and inappropriate dealings with his models, she wondered why he had changed. She was never told. Instead he had turned his attention to the one thing he craved and knew he could control. Phoenix. He needed her devotion and dependence on him in order to remain strong. Walter was always determined not to let her go.

The car slowly pulled up to Mr. Chow's on 57th street. Phoenix flung open her door before the driver could come around and open it for her. "Sorry," she waved to him

apologetically. She tried to calm the nerves in her stomach by

quickly reapplying her lipstick and putting on her best I-am-

here-for-business face. As she walked into the restaurant she

immediately spotted the table of Mr. Stiles who look

extremely gentle and joyous in a signature black suit and

diamond earrings. She hadn't noticed it before but it looked

like he was growing out his slightly curled black hair. His five

o' clock shadow gave him a rugged charm. She hadn't quite

noticed it earlier, but seeing him gently rub his jaws definitely

brought it to her attention. She imagined rubbing her lips

against it and down to his neck.

Phoenix was hesitant in her approach to the table.

She didn't know how she would react if Dexter tried to

reenact the scene that had occurred at his offices earlier in the day. The way she was feeling she may not be able to resist his advances. She felt a knot stirring in her stomach as she approached the table and realized that there were only four chairs and everyone was paired up someone. She stood frozen within a few feet of the table. "Are you ok Miss?" asked one of the waiters placing a hand on her shoulder. "Ugh, yes, I am looking for the restroom," she said. "Of course, it's straight down the hall to the left."

"Thank you," she said shielding her face with her clutch and walking towards the restroom. She needed to assess the situation and she couldn't do it by standing in front of Dexter and his dinner party. Phoenix slipped into the restroom and called Laila. Laila groggily answered on the fourth ring. "What's up girl?"

"Hey La, look I am sorry to bother you. You sound a little busy, but look I am here at Mr. Chow's-"

"With who?" Laila asked.

"I'm here to meet Dexter-"

"Dexter who?" Laila asked sounding suspicious.

"Dexter Stiles-"

"Dexter Stiles! What are you meeting him for?" Phoenix felt that this conversation was going to open up a can of worms if she didn't hurry up and nip it in the bud. "Look Laila, I can't really talk so listen. Dexter invited me here but he is at the table with three other people. There isn't an extra chair and I don't know what to do?"

"Well who is he with?" she asked.

"I don't know. Two girls and a guy-"

"Look, I can come up there if you want and we can meet with Dexter together. I mean we have some friends in common and that may make it easier for you to approach him so you won't have to be by yourself." Phoenix shook her head. It was getting late and she wanted to hurry and get this over with. Waiting on Laila to come and possibly pitch her company during a business meeting was not going to work.

"No girl, you just rest up or go back to doing what you were doing. I can handle this. I'll just call you in the morning or something."

"Ok Phoenix," she said sounding disappointed. "You know I am here for you if you need me. If you need me to come down I can get ready quick so just let me know. I love Mr. Chow's it's one of my favorite spots."

"Thanks girl, I know you have my back. I am going to get in there. I will talk to you tomorrow." She hung up the phone and walked out the bathroom. She didn't know who was at the table but she knew that she had been invited and that was all that mattered.

Dexter looked pensive as he sipped his Perrier. On his left was a gorgeous woman in a red silk dress draped in what looked like all the diamonds she owned kept rubbing his shoulders and trying to purr in his ear. As Phoenix got closer to the table she recognized the man sitting across from the woman as Willie Escobando, editor in chief of Flashy magazine. Next to him was the actress Jennifer Harper looking sleepy and intoxicated. Her ample breasts spilled from her shirt as she sucked the olives from her dry Martini and listened to Dexter and Willie talk about the new

campaign that was to kick off inside the pages of Flashy.

"I want the spread to be hot," Dexter said. "The girl

that is representing DQS Style has got to be different. Not

just beautiful she got to be different, like something that

other people are gonna say…wow…where did they find her.

You know what I'm saying? A fresh face that is accessible and

universal at the same time. You know what I'm saying?"

Willie nodded his head in agreement. He had been

friends with Dexter since their young days on the block and

to see him so focused and into excited about his new

Cosmetic Line. DQS Style was exciting to watch.

"I mean, this girl is basically the face of the line. With

DQS Style Cosmetics, I am trying to give women of color a

way to look beautiful and natural and enhanced. Not

intensified you know what I'm saying?"

Lisa cleared her throat, her own make-up thick enough for

the stage.

"I mean think about it how many times have you walked up

to a woman in the club, she was looking sexy right? You

stared at her in the eye, rubbed her face a little and it was

crazy what was on your hand. Like a clown's. I understand

that women need the makeup. You have to have it because

you have to be pulled together, and DQS Cosmetics is giving

you that. It has a water base its natural, it's a good product.

That's what I needed to see and we created it." Dexter waved

his chopsticks in the air emphasizing with his chicken the

seriousness of the matter.

"Like look at Jennifer over there? I've seen Jennifer with like a clown mask on before. It's ridiculous."

"Here we go," Jennifer said rising her martini glass to her lips spilling a little.

"Why you always got to use me as an example?" Dexter fixed his eyes on her as he watched her down the last of her drink.

"I saw you at the Oscars and you were something crazy on the red carpet. You win best supporting actress and you looked like a white *man* on the red carpet. The make-up didn't match your complexion. That's why I told you that you need some black representation. You need someone to give you the right direction because the streets aren't buying it."

Jennifer shrunk into herself as she flagged the waiter over and asked for a refill on her cocktail.

"Forget the streets Dexter. The streets don't pay my bills. The streets didn't win my Academy Award. Forget the damn streets. Look I need to pee," she said getting up from the table. "Dexter you really need to learn to respect people truly. I respect your game and therefore you need to respect mine. I work too hard and I know what I'm doing." Her brown eyes looked wounded under her furrowed brow. It was bad enough that she had allowed herself to be used as Dexter's side piece in the past and he had brutally used her and cast her aside for Lisa Whitaker, but she didn't need to be disrespected too.

This was a normal thing from Dexter lately. She didn't know how Lisa put up with it. Maybe because his mom was ill in the hospital with cancer he had become particularly evil and unfriendly. Lisa looked over at Dexter who had returned to his conversation with Willie about the direction

of the DQS line.

"Like I was saying, the model that becomes the face

of the cosmetic line is going to have to outdo what Lisa did

for the fashion line kick off," Dexter said-eyes roaming over

Lisa's body like a piece of property. "Honestly Lisa I think

that unfortunately we saturated your face in the market and

now they're wondering what you're going to do next. Some

people say they need a break from you for a while so you can

reemerge as a megastar again, you know."

Lisa looked at him eyes blaring. "What do you mean by *do*

next? I'm the face DQS Style Fashion. That's what I do.

That's how we built the brand with my image." Dexter

looked at her sternly.

"Actually Lisa, I built this brand and you were lucky enough to get on it. What I am saying is right now the brand needs more than that. I need more than that. I need you to change. Do something. Have a baby. Let's do maternity fashion or something. I need more." Lisa rolled her eyes and took out her compact and checked her make up.

"She is a star Dexter," Willie said coming to Lisa's defense. "You just said that her face was saturating the market. So which is it? You're confusing me," he laughed. "Yeah Dexter you're so confusing, perhaps you need to decide what you want," Lisa said. "Oh I know what I want," Dexter said grabbing her thigh and smiling. Lisa pushed his hands away as he blew her a kiss.

She was so tired of Dexter and his demands. He wanted more and she knew exactly what he meant by that. He wanted her to carry on his legacy yet he wouldn't tie the knot and marry her. How was she ever supposed to be anything if he constantly beat her down the way he did lately?

"I think I am going to go and join Jennifer," Lisa said getting up from the table.

"Be sure to save some of that ass for me later Lis. Don't give it all to Jennifer," he said laughing. "Go to hell Dexter," she said. Lisa stormed off brusquely bumping into Phoenix as she made her way to the restroom.

Phoenix walked over to Dexter's table and stood at the edge.

"Hello Dexter," she said flashing her best smile. Dexter's eyes lit up as he looked her over. "Oh hey," Dexter said rising to give her a kiss on the cheek. "I'm glad you could make it. Really glad," he said smiling a bright smile.

"I wouldn't miss it for the world," she said.

"You look nice. I like the dress. Simple," he said.

"I'm glad you approve. I picked it specifically with you in mind."

"Is that right?" He said smiling sheepishly with approval. Dexter and Phoenix broke their gaze when Phoenix cleared her throat. "I'm sorry Phoenix, let me introduce you to my friend. This is Willie Esobando. I've known him ever since we were young knuckle heads on the block. He is-"

"The editor in chief of Flashy Magazine," Phoenix said. "I recognize your face from the magazine. Nice to meet you Willie." Willie gave her a warm smile and nodded in approval. "Nice to meet you too."

"Have a seat next to me," Dexter said patting the vacant chair beside him.

"Where did the ladies go?" she asked.

"Don't worry about that. Have a seat," Dexter said.

Phoenix slid into the padded chair and looked around the restaurant. It was beautiful and filled with beautiful people.

"You want some food?" Willie asked.

"Sure. I am here for dinner right?" she asked trying not to sound too eager.

"Well, we always like to ask. I know you know models like to watch your weight."

"Not this model," Phoenix said reaching for a pot sticker. "A girl's got to eat to stay alive right?"

"See Willie, I told you she was a winner. Help yourself sweetheart. Anyway, as I was saying to Willie before you joined us Phoenix, is that we are really going take our time with DQS Cosmetics because we aren't just making make-up for ladies to paint their faces with. We plan to become what the urban market looks to for style. We desire to be the

standard of beauty. This is a multi-million dollar campaign

that I am putting together. It's something that I wanted to do

for a long time. I want to break away from music and

reinvent myself as kind of a modern day Estee Lauder for the

urban market. That's why I am casting the everyday woman.

We want a woman who is accessible and beautiful; but with a

background and story that is truly inspirational and American.

We lost the dream baby and I'm trying to get it back.

Whoever becomes spokes model of this elite brand of

cosmetics will be paid a sum that will change their whole

lifestyle," Dexter turned and looked at Phoenix's face.

Her eyes seemed to grow at the sound of changing

her lifestyle. He laughed to himself as he she attempted to

keep a straight face and prevent herself from smiling. Her

front was hopeless. He could smell her hunger for fame and fortune.

"Sounds wonderful Mr. Stiles. It seems like any girl that is lucky enough to become your spokes model is going to have a huge responsibility as not only a role model but in building a brand name and inspiring the youth. I mean, I don't want to come off as too aggressive but I would love to be a part of this great vision that you have." Dexter laughed he wasn't used to models being so formal. He found Phoenix's courteous manner endearing.

"Mr. Stiles? Baby this is family. Call me Dexter. No one calls me Mr. Stiles unless I am about to spend a lot of money in their establishment." He pulled out his phone and typed while speaking. "So what do you think of her face Will?"

"I think she's gorgeous. Sexy. Nice features. Possibly DQS Cosmetics."

"Yeah, but can she be the face of this line?"

"I mean we would have to do some test shoots to be sure," Willie said.

"Test shots? She's going to look great she's an actress. You don't remember her from that show All for One? It was a good show. They canceled it too quick though. I remember watching it and thinking ok, she has a little something." They all laughed.

"Well that was a long time ago," Phoenix smiled bashfully. The men seemed to study her face as she Phoenix sought of a way to make herself more attractive for the offer.

"Well I used to model a few years ago too. I have a book. My boyfriend was a photographer so I have some shots and I

116

also did some things in Paris. I mean, Paris didn't work out like I had planned but-"

"Yeah, you're a little short for Paris," Dexter said. "But print you should be all right."

"How long ago was that?" Willie said. "I'm pretty familiar with editorials. I mean I see so many girls though. You kind of look vaguely familiar but I can't recall." Phoenix looked down at her plate. "Well, it was three years ago," she said. "And it was small stuff so if you blinked you may have missed it. I was just trying to get my feet wet and then my representation fell through and then it got really crazy. It's a long story," she said nervously.

"Well a lot changes in three years," Dexter said. "You were how old then 22? No offense you were old then. Now you're what twenty-eight? I mean that's ancient in modeling years. Hell Lisa's almost ancient. I told her she needed to re-invent do the mom thing, but she don't have any foresight. She just wants to be an ingénue forever and that's not only boring, but impossible."

"Yeah, but Phoenix looks barely twenty. She could pass for a teenager if she wanted to," Willie said. The two men kept on discussing her as if she were not at the table. Phoenix felt her head getting light with this conversation. Dexter was so hard to read. She wasn't sure by the way he talked if he was interested in her abilities or not. Phoenix vowed to play it cool no matter what. What she did know was that this campaign could take her to the level that she wanted to go, but with all of his criticisms she wondered why he was even interested if he thought that she was so subpar.

The waiter came by to bring her green tea. The men continued to talk amongst themselves. Phoenix tried to stay active in the conversation as she drank her tea. She was feeling sort of out of place with the likes of Mr. Stiles. He was a major media mogul that seemed to possibly want her for his campaign but had questioned her worth and credibility from the moment they met.

Dexter Stiles was an imposing figure. She has noticed his presence everywhere in New York. Everywhere she turned she seemed to be faced with his imagine or some extension of it in magazines, on the runway, and at his restaurant. This was a moment that she had worked hard for, for many years and now it was staring her in the face. The realization of possibly obtaining her dreams overwhelmed her, and she found herself doubting if she was ready to move amongst the true power players of New York City. Phoenix glanced over at Willie Escobando. Willie had the gentlest face. His smooth olive skin created the perfect palate for a his black marble eyes that seemed to transfer the sensitivity from his soul onto Phoenix as he watched her struggle to maintain her position in the formidable presence of Dexter. His presence made Phoenix feel comfortable and she had a slight feeling that Willie would become a good friend to her.

"Phoenix, I love your face I think it's beautiful," Willie said giving her a wink. "I think it's fresh and more importantly I like your vibe I think it's refreshing. That's how stars are made. People feel like they can get close to them or somehow become that person."

"Outside of DQS Cosmetics, I would like to test you out with one of the photo shoots we have coming up," he said.

"Wow," Phoenix said. "I expected to have to grovel at your feet or something," she laughed. "No, none of that. I think you would be good for this shoot. You fit the profile plus you are a friend of Dex's so I don't mind helping out. Anyway, there is a new artist that's making some noise right about now named Big City. He's a young dude out of Detroit and he is making some waves with his new company Fearless Entertainment." Dexter sat up in his chair, tossing his ear piece out of his ear; and began banging the table in agitation.

"You mean to tell me that fool is coming out? I thought I shut him down permanently. He's horrible. No woman that may represent my company should come within inches of that clown. Are you working with him Willie?" Dexter asked. Willie shrugged his shoulders.

"What? I have to do my job man. He is creating buzz, what am I supposed to do?" Dexter shook his head at Willie.

"Willie, Big City has no respect. He comes into the game and thinks that he is going take my title and my empire, all off of one or two hit records and a startup clothing line and record label? Do you know he actually told people this nonsense and then tried to barge into my event? After all I've done for him he disrespects me like this. Unreal. It never will happen as long as I can help it."

Willie shook his head looking at Dexter as he continued to mutter to himself and check his messages. Dexter had been hearing a lot from the infamous Big City who was claiming to not only be the best rapper in the game but was rising up a new empire in the music industry that was going to make more noise and become and formidable force in the industry that was comparable to DQS."

Willie, ignoring Dexter and his usual tirades, directed his attention towards Phoenix.

"Like I said Phoenix, we are doing a spread on Big City because he is making noise in the music industry. He is a young guy and he does have a hit single out and he just signed a huge distribution deal with Interscope Records. He has new artists coming out. Movies."

"I told you not to talk about that fool around me!" screamed Dexter. "Are you kidding me? Who is Big City? Nobody knew who he was until I showed him around. Willie, you know this. This is some crap."

"I know Dex, but my job is to present what's hot to my readers and City is hot right now."

"Yeah, whatever man," Dexter said slipping on his sunglasses. He needed to think and he no longer felt like he wanted to be a part of the conversation. What he did feel however, were the pangs of his mortality shooting through is chest as he pondered his dealings with Big City. He recalled the time when he too was a young and hungry entrepreneur eager to start his career and to make a difference in his life.

There was nothing that was going to stop him. Dexter was determined to see his name in lights along the genteel streets of Manhattan that had frequently denied him access during his childhood. No one was going to stand in his way from success. He and Big City had beef and he wasn't going to forget it. It was business between the two but it was beginning to feel personal.

"Anyway, Phoenix," Willie said. "Let me give you my info I think you would be hot for the spread, come by the office and we'll talk. Let me take a look at your book and we'll go from there. What we're trying to do is create a Casino theme with Big City as the Robert DeNiro character but we're probably going to do this within the next couple of weeks."

Phoenix felt her heart stretch and flutter up above Mr. Chow's as she thought about appearing in Flashy magazine a job on her own accord.

"What's up with you trying to steal my model from me Willie?"

Phoenix looked over at Dexter who looked threatened.

125

"Oh, now I'm your model? I thought perhaps I wasn't hot enough to represent DQS Cosmetics according to you," Phoenix said with a smile.

Dexter turned to face her smiling. He started to say something, but Phoenix had already seized her moment and began to answer Willie who looked at the pair smiling.

"Yes Willie, here is my number," she said, the two exchanging info.

"Let's meet. I love your magazine and working with Big City sounds like something that I would love to do."

"Well its set then."

Dexter turned back to his food. He felt like something had been stolen from him although it hadn't been. Dexter brought himself back from his thoughts quickly enough to discover an annoyed Lisa standing over him.

"Well well well, Dexter, I leave for a few minutes to take care of a friend and you already got somebody sitting in my seat," Lisa's eyes were cold as she looked around at the table. A visibly startled Phoenix ceased her side conversation with Willie to look up into the face of the Lisa Whitaker. Dexter had done a lot of things but she was positive that she had run everywoman that stood in her way out of Dexter's life as of late. Lisa tried her best to hide her obvious disgust at the woman sitting in her seat. She didn't know this woman but she immediately felt threatened. Lisa knew that Dexter enjoyed his trashy girls but he would never stay with them, but this one was different, she was not your typical bottom feeder.

"I'm so sorry, I can give you your seat back," Phoenix said half-heartedly rising to stand. There was so much written on Lisa's face that Phoenix was unsure how she would act if she remained seated. Lisa stood motionless as she waited for Phoenix to rise from her seat. Dexter smiled at the women's unspoken territorial exchange at the table. Lisa broke her eyes away briefly to address her man who she felt loved this awkward situation way too much.

"You were gone so long Lisa I didn't think you were coming back. You left 45 minutes ago," Dexter laughed.

"I'm always coming back Dexter, remember that," Lisa said her eyes looking at Phoenix. "I can't believe I can't leave you for one minute," she said reaching across Phoenix for her drink.

Phoenix hurried out of the seat and let Lisa slide in next to Dexter. Lisa tried to rub his cheek as she leaned in for a kiss. Dexter turned away, not wanting to be touched by her.

Her face looked wounded as she motioned for the waiter to clear Phoenix's plates from in front of her. Phoenix stood at the edge of the table with an uncomfortable smile plastered on her face. She hated how the once open and receptive table had now been closed off to her all because Dexter's woman felt a sense of entitlement.

The waiter cleared the plates as if he didn't notice that Phoenix was standing, or that she even had been sitting there before the woman had come back. Phoenix was all too familiar with this type of drill. She was always nice to look at and fun to be around until the real celebrities or the more highly paid or working models came around. That's when

Phoenix noticed that the girls became extremely catty and territorial and catty and the men played right into their hands. It was times like those that drove Phoenix every day.

She wanted the respect that the other women had because they were accomplished and she was determined to get it.

A newly refreshed and alert Jennifer slid into the chair next to Willie and began to whisper in his ear. Willie was now smiling to himself as Jennifer and her long red fingernails made their way up Willie's jeans and onto his crotch. Inspired by the heat of the moment Dexter pulled Lisa's chair closer to him and kissed her half-heartedly on her cheek. A small reluctant smile spread across her face. Phoenix stuck her clutch under her arm, shifting her weight onto her left foot as she looked down in embarrassment. She scratched her head as she stepped out of the way letting the waiter pass in front of her to fill the water glasses. She was all for sticking it out through the hard times but this was ridiculous. She knew this was supposed to be strictly professional but seeing the two of them kiss was turning her stomach, especially when thoughts of Dexter's lips coming within inches of her own kept running through her mind.

"Well, it was nice meeting all of you," Phoenix said. Her voice barely resonated over the din of the restaurant and onto the small group that stood a few feet from her. Dexter looked up momentarily from the ecstasy he was experiencing from Lisa kissing his neck to wave to Phoenix.

"Thanks for coming, get home safe. I already handled the car," Dexter said. She could have been mistaken but she thought she saw a devilish grin of satisfaction on Dexter's face as he dismissed her. Phoenix was incredulous that after all of his coercing her to meet him at the restaurant he hadn't even asked her to pull up an extra cab or offer his car service for her to get home safely.

"Unbelievable," she muttered. "I'll take a cab Dexter thank you. Willie, I'll call you this week."
Willie was caught in a slow and seductive lip lock, but managed to raise his hand and wave a feeble good-bye.

She turned on her heels and left in silence as the table carried on without her.

She stood in the front of Mr. Chow's her brown eyes feeling misty. *Oh my gosh*, she thought, *Am I feeling sad or something? For what?* She stepped out onto the curb past the pretentious dinners that were nonchalantly climbing in and out of luxury vehicles as they entered and exited the restaurant. She hated the way that the valet staff and management pandered to the patrons yet she knew if she were in their position she would be more gracious. Even worse she had no idea where the car was Dexter mentioned and she would have to stand to the side and try to hail a cab. She stuck her hand out and almost immediately a cab pulled up.

She looked inside of her purse and saw that she only had a few dollars on her and decided to let the cab pass her by. Phoenix felt the gravity of the night pull her shoulders towards the ground. Although she didn't want to be smothered by Dexter, she didn't want to be shut out by him either. She felt so small compared to the group. Lisa especially. She sauntered over to Dexter as if she were the queen bee of the room with all of her jewelry flashing. Dexter must have bought that for her, she thought. Phoenix wondered if Lisa's life was anything like hers when she was with Walter. Probably not. Lisa seemed to be stronger and more assertive than she ever was.

Phoenix looked up at the night sky and sighed, a sense of exasperation overtaking her, as she began to look for the car that Dexter had sent for her. She didn't want his handouts but she really didn't have a choice. She reached for her cellphone to call inside the restaurant and have them locate Dexter so that she could locate the car. The maître D informed her that had already left as she turned around to see him and his crew coming through the doors of the restaurant.

Lisa's had her arm locked territorially around Dexter's while he vehemently continued his conversation on his phone. Lisa looked smug as she stared straight ahead past the staff that was clearly fawning over the foursome.

Willie and Jennifer remained in their own world as he ravenously massaged her behind. The tiny valet staffer ran over to Dexter and handed him his keys. Dexter thanked him the man with a warm smile and peeled off a stack of bills that nearly had the man bowing at his feet. As the crew piled into the car, Dexter noticed Phoenix standing in front of the restaurant trying to look inconspicuous and shot her a confused look.

Phoenix waved a weak goodbye as if to hurry him along. Dexter responded with a smile. Phoenix nervously tapped her foot and prayed that Dexter's car would pull off but it didn't. She turned to walk down the street when suddenly Dexter exited the car and ran over to her.

"You alright?" he said.

"Yeah, I'm fine," Phoenix said. "You ok?"

135

Dexter looked concerned. "You were supposed to be long gone. I thought you were getting into the car I sent?"

"Yes that was nice but I was going to grab a cab but it looks like I misplaced my money," she said averting her eyes and looking arbitrarily through her purse. "My wallet was stolen recently so I am not used to carrying this purse…"

Dexter watched her mouth and smiled knowingly as she began to fumble through her story about her wallet and not getting a car. She tossed her hair over her shoulders and fiddled with her back and rambled out her story. For the first time she seemed to lose the tough act and appeared nervous around him. Dexter muted out her words as he stared into her eyes.

"So Dexter, that's why I am still here," she shrugged. "So, ugh, where is the car you hired for me? Is it still available by chance?"

He stuck his hands in his pockets and leaned in close to her. "Well if you're not claustrophobic anymore baby girl, you can ride with me. My mother didn't raise me to leave beautiful women stranded in the middle of the night." She looked into his eyes thankful that he didn't blow her cover.

"Thank you," she said exhaling. "But wait, what about Lisa? Will she mind that you have another woman in your car? She seemed like she eats women for dinner if they get too close."

"I wouldn't worry about that. That's my ride and you're with me. Besides you're a model and she knows the difference. Shall we? " he said holding out his arm to her. She grabbed it allowing a grateful smile to escape from her lips as they walked to the car.

Phoenix already felt the tension as she saw a somber Lisa sitting with her face towards the window. Lisa didn't turn to acknowledge Phoenix. Phoenix started to speak but thought better of it when she heard Lisa sniffle as if she was desperately trying to fight back the tears. Dexter slide in next to Phoenix and put his arm around her. "Dexter c'mon now, you're doing too much," Jennifer pleaded. Dexter silenced her with his hand and Jennifer rubbed her friend's lap.

"Now folks let's get this money," Dexter shouted. "That's what I want to do. I want to get this money! Willie, I'm going to be narrowing down my final model over the next week or so and we can anticipate a fall release date. Get all the back to school girls, kids and mom's getting ready for that fall season change, you know? And you know what's even better? I may have already found my new model right here. She has such as fresh new face. Plus she seems like a good girl."

Lisa grabbed a small blue pill case from her purse and popped two of the white pills in her mouth. She leaned back in the seat and closed her eyes.

"Let me get one too," Jennifer said. "What is that?"

Dexter's eyes narrowed as he watched Lisa. He hated when she popped pills. He didn't even want to ask her what she was taking this time. She would only say that they were some kind of pain or happy pill anyway. She seemed to be popping a lot of pills these days. He rubbed his hands along his jaw line and fixed his icy stare fixed on Lisa.

"Lisa," he said shaking her shoulders. "You're being rude to my guests wake up. Did you introduce yourself to Phoenix?" Lisa forced a smile as she extended her hand. "Hi, Phoenix you're *very* gorgeous. I noticed that when I first saw you. Dexter likes that. He likes gorgeous little women." Her eyes seemed almost defeated as she spoke. "One word of advice to you honey. Be *very* careful."

She gave a reluctant smile to Phoenix and instructed the driver to let her off uptown. She wasn't going to sit and be humiliated any longer by Dexter and his ingénue whose naïve act was beginning to bore her. If Dexter wanted to cast her to the side he could she knew that he would come back like always did. If she wasn't so tired she would slap that goofy grin he had on his face when he looked at Phoenix. The car couldn't pull over quick enough for her.

140

"Well gang, this is my stop." She said gathering her things and looking at Dexter who was now engaged with his phone.

"I assume you will be hard at work and not coming home tonight?" Lisa asked

"I'm always working baby." He said not looking up. Phoenix tried to slide away from Dexter sensing an eruption between the two. Lisa departed from the car as if this were her last time seeing the light of day.

"Of course, how else are you going to be so rich and successful right?" she said exiting the car. She poked her head in one final time to see Phoenix.

"Nice meeting you Phoenix, I hope you get the campaign. It'll change your life and then some. And remember I told you, be very careful there's always strings attached. Working with Dexter is quite an experience. He plays to win."

Dexter stopped his call and sneered at Lisa. "Good night Lisa, shut the door. We don't want to hear your philosophical bullshit right now, be good," he said waving his hand at her to hurry up as he gripped the handle of the door pulling it closed.

Jennifer was passed out in Willie's arm as the car rolled toward the Upper Westside. The night was cool and Phoenix felt Dexter's arm pull her closer by her waist next to him. His hands felt so strong and she felt herself sink into his touch. The car forged on into the night in silence. Phoenix looked up at Dexter's strong face and a feeling of fear and excitement rushed through her. Dexter softly stroked her cheek with his finger. Phoenix closed her eyes as he gently explored her face. This was supposed to be a professional

relationship and she didn't want to feel as if she was falling so

fast but she couldn't help it. There was an undeniable

electricity and familiarity between them that both of them

felt. She knew that they were somehow supposed to be in

each other's lives but she just didn't know how. Dexter didn't

say a word as he laid her head on his shoulder and rubbed her

hair. She knew that she was crossing some dangerous lines

and wanted to pull her head away from him, but she stayed

feeling his slow and steady breath on her forehead.

Dexter tilted her head towards him as he slowly

kissed her lips. Phoenix let out a soft groan and fell limp in

his arms. The kiss went on for what seemed like eternity until

the car pulled over to the side of the road to drop off Willie

and Jennifer. Willie hopped out giving Dexter a pound and

maneuvering the sleepy Jennifer out by her waist. As soon as Willie and Jennifer left the car he turned his attention back on Phoenix, gently rubbing her lips with his finger. Man, you have the softest lips I have ever kissed. I feel like I can't stop kissing you," he said grabbing her face and devouring her lips. They both began laughing when they realized their lips were sore. "This is like high school or something," Dexter said gazing into her eyes. "You're special and beautiful." Phoenix silenced him with a kiss as they lied down onto the back seat.

The night was beginning to feel surreal as the car navigated the city. Every time the driver wanted to make a stop Dexter told him to keep driving so that he could spend more time with her. Phoenix was beginning to feel like Cinderella at the ball with Dexter, her prince, showing her his world. This was an exclusive world of money, power and opportunity, and Phoenix was getting to experience it with one of the sweetest men she had ever met. He was the king of New York and she was riding in the car with him. She let a sigh of relief escape from her lips as she felt a sense of safety from Dexter's gentle rubbing of her arm.

Phoenix turned to Dexter and looked into his searching eyes.

"Thank you," she said.

"For what?"

"Taking care of me."

He kissed her forehead and rubbed his finger over her nose and ending with a gently pinch on her chin as he smiled.

"You remind me of my mother."

Phoenix was taken aback by his words. That was the last thing she expected to hear coming from his mouth.

"How did you come to that conclusion?" she asked.

"Because, you both are beautiful people with beautiful spirits."

"Dexter," Phoenix said pulling away from him. "Look, I'm not who you think I am. I'm not what you think I am. I'm not some angel reincarnated; I am just a girl who is out here trying to make it."

"We are all out here trying to make it. But I still believe that you are everything I think you are. You're probably more than I think you are. I didn't get to be in the position I'm in by being a bad judge of character," he said kissing her on the lips. An ocean of warmth washed over her. She wanted to tell him to stop so that she could stop the butterflies in her stomach but she felt dizzy when he pulled away.

"It's a brand new day in New York. I can feel it," he said. The pair effortlessly laughed with each other as Dexter told her stories of his childhood and the antics he and his brother Wade got into in Brooklyn. Phoenix admired his strong sense of family and listened in awe as she sat before such a powerful man who presented himself as just a regular guy. Yet Phoenix knew these feelings all too well. In the past she had been drawn to the paternal nature of Walter and immediately recognized the same attributes in Dexter.

Although this time she knew that she had a goal in mind and her mind drifted back to thoughts about the campaign. Phoenix put her fingers over Dexter's lips to get his attention.

"Hey," she said.

"What?" Dexter said. "I'm chatting more than a female right now huh?"

"No, that's not it. I could ride around with you all night but I should probably get back. I have a meeting in the morning."

"Cancel it," he said. "You are rolling with the best right now. What could be more important than this?"

Phoenix laughed. "Oh just cancel it huh? Look, I can't just blow off my obligations. I'm not like that. I stay committed. Plus people put a lot of effort into getting me these meetings. Everyone isn't big time like you Dexter Stiles."

"Who is the meeting with?" he said. "I bet I know him."

"It's a test shoot with a photographer for a magazine spread," she said. "I mean if it's a go they are going to definitely use the photos and I was told that more than likely they would."

"What magazine?"

"Wide Open magazine."

148

"That trash rag? You think you're going to pose for Wide Open magazine?"

"Wide Open Magazine has made a lot of girls famous Dexter, and right now, I could use the exposure. You know the game is all about exposure and I am trying to get my name out there in the industry."

"And you think having dudes looking at spreads with your ass on motorcycles is going make you hot?"

"Look at Jennifer Lopez. She started out in videos."

"Jennifer Lopez is a trained dancer. If you're trying to model your career after video chicks, than you don't need me to help you with that. I don't really operate with people at that level. I'm trying to make a real change an impact. You are thinking way too small. You got to think bigger than that."

"Look, Joe Malone at Wide Open is feeling me; he saw my acting reel and my modeling portfolio and said that I could do a lot of things with them. He believed in me and he never questioned if I was hot enough, he saw it right away and wanted to set something up. Look you're established. I'm not. I just want to get my face and image out there." Dexter looked over her withdrawing his arm.

"Wide Open magazine," he muttered.

"What Dexter? Its work, what do you care? You act as if I'm your girl and it's going to ruin your reputation."

"Well, do you think I want the face of DQS Cosmetics up showcasing her ass in a semi-porn magazine calling herself an actress among all the other video bitches they got spread out on the pages. Get real? That's not classy and you're not going to look classy in it."

"They're going to pay me Dexter, I need to work. What do you expect? I'm just supposed to hold out for my contract with you."

Dexter felt his face grow hot. Maybe she was not who he thought she was.

"Oh, okay," he said taking out his wallet. "Here's 1000 dollars cash," he said tossing the money on her lap. "Isn't that about how much you'll make spreading your ass in Wide Open magazine right. Here take it. You need the money. You're already doing Flashy that's not enough for you?"

Phoenix picked the money from her lap tossed it back in his face.

"I can't believe you just did that. I don't need or want your fucking money. You can't buy me and I can do whatever I want." Phoenix sat up and sat completely opposite from him. "Driver, drop me off at the next block please. I have to get out the car. It's starting to stink."

"No you don't driver, we're going uptown," he shouted.

"No driver, I'm going downtown."

They squared off in silence.

"How long you are you going to play this stupid game. I know you struggling, you not hiding it very well. You had your little sugar daddy Walter Deveroux, the faded out photographer give you up with nice gifts and now he's gone and you trying to get on with the A-Team. I'm trying to put you on and you playing me like I'm a sucker and I'm not going for it." He tapped his finger angrily against the window.

"You know you needed that grand baby," he said. "You want to pose for Wide Open go ahead you'll be right where you belong. You'll fit right in with the rest of the hoes."

The car pushed on through the night as if moving through molasses. Phoenix felt as if she were caught in a time capsule as she listened to Dexter hurl insults at her.

"You're right, you're not who I thought you were. I thought you were a lady."

"I am lady. But you're not acting like a man, right now. You're acting more like an asshole."

Phoenix fought back the tears. Dexter's cold mood sent chills up her spine. He went from warm kisses to ice cold insults. All she wanted to do was prove was that she could make a name for herself. She thought it would impress him, not

153

anger him that she had sought out work for herself. That was not the case.

The driver pulled over in front of the Sotho Grand. Phoenix quickly gathered her things as she quickly got out.

He went to reach for her arm as she pulled away.

"You may talk to your other women like that, but not me. I'm just trying to make a living for myself."

Dexter looked like a small boy as she got out of the car to leave.

"Look, Phoenix, it just bothers me that someone with your talent and beauty would want to do some shit like that."

"I have to go Dexter." He inched closer to the door to stop her.

"Just stay with me tonight," he pleaded. "Why stay at a hotel?"

She felt a tug at her heart when he asked her to stay. The warmth of his hands sent a surge through her body. "No, Dexter. I have a meeting I told you. And it's getting late."

He let her arm go as he pushed her away from the door and shut it. Phoenix watched the car as it drove away. She was bewildered at what happened. She stood watching the car drive all the way into the night before she went in through the doors of the SoHo grand and retired to her room.

Dexter unlocked the doors to his Upper West Side Apartment. The white carpeting of the foyer seemed to stretch for miles into the living. The house was silent and cold as if no one had lived there in months. The crystal vases glistened and sparkled from the white tables they sat on. He

155

tossed his keys on the white divan as he crept back into the

bedroom to look for Lisa. He had done this many times,

fighting with her, and going to make up with her. He looked

in the master bedroom. The bed was still flawless. He shut

off the lights and made his way down the hall to the guest

bedroom where she sometimes slept when they were fighting.

The room droned in the silence of the air conditioning. No

Lisa. His heart raced wondering where she was. He had

dropped her off and hour ago. He went up the winding stairs

to the family room and terrace. He noticed a half finished

drink and a pack of cigarettes lying on the bar. He stepped

out into the breeze of the terrace. His heart fell as he realized

she was not there. He called her on his cellphone. She did not

answer. He called her back and her phone went straight to

voiced mail. He pulled up her number and sent her a quick message. *Where are you??*

He waited a moment for the reply that never came. He didn't know where she was and at that moment he didn't have the energy to care. He walked back into the house and went downstairs to his master bedroom. He took off his clothes, the warmth of his pants feeling the chill of the crisp bed sheets. He rarely spent time here. He lied back under the covers and reached for the remote control. As he clicked the blank channels in vain, frustrated, he tossed the remote onto the floor realizing that the cable bill had not been paid. How could the bill not be paid? Every month he moved $55,000 through his household. And his bill wasn't paid. Lisa comes here almost every night and she didn't inform him of this. He jumped out of bed. Black Calvin Klein boxers hugging his muscular thighs and went into the kitchen for juice. He found

no juice, but there were plenty of bottles of champagne and

cheese and energy drinks. *Where is the food in this house?* He shut

the refrigerator door and shut off the lights. I come home

and there's no food? There's nothing but liquor in this house.

He did not want to be there. It felt cold and empty. He

wanted to be with Phoenix, he wanted to be with Lisa. Hell,

he wanted to be with somebody. With all the women he knew

in New York City he was spending the night alone. He

opened the window and allowed the light from the moon to

come in. He had an early day tomorrow. There were two

meetings, a lunch and then a dinner. He hoped Lisa knew the

schedule and knew that they needed to be on tomorrow for

the Viacom meeting concerning the line. His mind trailed to

Phoenix and their previous encounter.

For some reason Phoenix posing for Wide Open magazine was really getting under his skin. He wanted her right next to him. Right up under his arm. And she was being stubborn. He didn't want to leave her like that. Her face look wounded when he shut the door on her, but that's how it felt when she left out and said that she was posing for that trash rag. He rolled onto his back, placing his hands behind his head as he stared at the ceiling.

Chapter Six

Big City was making moves. There was no denying that. Fearless Entertainment had just purchased two floors in the office building next to his on Fifth Avenue. He was only twenty-seven years old and he was already buying major property. It took Dexter until he was thirty to make his money solid. Nowadays people came up from the streets with dirty money and turn it into something good. Start labels, sign their friends.

Big City had made it known time and time again that he wasn't going anywhere. Dexter could smell his hunger three years ago when he came in to his offices as a young artist looking for a deal and an A&R job. Dexter told him to choose. Big City stated cavalierly,

160

"I want it all man. I want to be you Dexter."

The look in his eye was crafty when he said it. Dexter could

see the greed burning behind his eyes. City didn't want to play

fair. Dexter wanted to keep him close nonetheless to see who

this kid was. He never knew he might come to heads with

him one day. He seemed thankful and eager to learn, yet

always quick with the interjections and the ideas. Dexter had

even overlooked the time he caught City sitting in the chair

behind his desk before a meeting fiddling with a cigar. He

loved his passion. His passion and ideas excited him. They

gave new blood to the company. He wanted that blood and

those ideas. But this kid wanted more than a job and a deal,

he wanted the empire. Word was beginning to spread that he

had been talking about Dexter and personal things about the

company. He was saying how Dexter didn't know what he was doing and the company was in the red.

It was true that in the past few years Dexter's record label had been experiencing some problems. However, that was something he was considering letting go because it wasn't really making him that much money. What really interested him was the thought of his lifestyle brand. That was what was going to really make his name great again. Dexter called his assistant Janet, "I'm on my way to see my mother. I need you to call Fearless and set up a conference with City and me."

Dexter opened the door to his mother's hospital room. Corrine Stiles lay limp and motionless in the bed. The soft buzz of machines filled the room. Radiation and chemotherapy had left her body weak but her face had an air of content even as she slept. Wade sat near her bedside holding her hand and occasionally placing a cool towel over her head.

Dexter hated seeing his mother this way. He was unable to handle seeing her lying in this bed lifeless. Her room was stocked with flowers her sheets lined in fine silk. He had special food prepared for her so that she wouldn't starve herself because she hated the hospital food, yet he never visited her. Seeing his mom lying there as is if she were a doped up fiend waiting to die angered him.

Wade had tried to impart to his brother the importance of visiting their mother. She asked for him every day and he always said that he was working or just too busy to come by. Wade knew better. Dexter had always been the closer one to Corrine Stiles and the most like their father. She had been a nurse herself and to think with all of her knowledge of health that she would be in a bed that she once used to maintain for patients was too ironic for Dexter. He was the responsible one. He had to go on. Let Wade handle mom his way, and Dexter would handle her his.

Wade watched as his mother stirred in her sleep and attempted to blink her eyes open. He had been sitting there for three days straight hoping that she would stay awake long enough to fully recognize him. Corrine had tossed and turned and mumbled things here and there. When she did speak she asked for her firstborn son.

Dexter had been avoiding his phone calls; claiming that he was too busy with the campaign. Wade loved and admired his older brother but often wished that he could be a little more sensitive. He often wondered what went wrong between them sometimes and what caused his brother to have an insatiable desire for success. He did notice that Dexter began to act even more strange when Wade married. Dexter was feeling threatened by the dynamic that Wade and Debra brought into to the family and it drew even more of a wedge between the brothers.

It was nearly 3:30 in the morning. It looked like it was going to be another long night. Wade laid his head on his mother's lap wishing that he could just curl up and fall asleep right between her bosom like he used to as a kid. Those

moments were gone now. He raised his head up from his

daydreams to see a somber Dexter standing before him hands

in pocket. He always did that when he was unsure of himself.

"Hey," Wade said. "What are you doing here?"

Dexter walked over slowly, his steps planned and careful, not

wanting to disrupt his mother's sleep. His eyes hallowed as he

walked over and kiss her forehead. Staying a moment to

breathe in her essence possibly trying to give a little of

himself to her.

"I couldn't sleep and I missed mom," he said. "I needed to

see her. How is she?"

"She is doing alright actually," Wade said. "Let me get you a

seat." He went and got him a seat. Wade looked at his

brother staring at their mother. He had known Dexter to be

one of the most fearless people that he knew; yet seeing their mother near death transported him back to their adolescence. Dexter blinked his eyes, trying to be inconspicuous by wiping his damp cheeks with the sleeve of his jacket

"How do you do it man?" Dexter said falling backwards into the brown chair. "How do you sit here every day?"

"Somebody's got too man, she's our mom."

Dexter felt his heart sinking he knew that his brother was trying to imply that he had not been there. Perhaps he hadn't been there physically in the hospital as much as he should but who was going to provide for the family? Dexter was supporting everyone on his back alone. He made it possible for his mother to be in the best hospital under the best care eating the best food. He fiddled with the wilting roses that lay next to his mother's bed.

"What's up with these flowers man, no one waters them or what?"

"They do Dexter, but they're dying, they're getting old."

"Yeah, well that's why you have to water them so that they will last longer. I send them so that when mom wakes up she can see them. Damn," he said putting his hands between his knees.

His brother was sensing a deeper problem in Dexter. He could tell by the look on his face when he came in the door that there was a deeper need and a deeper problem. Dexter breathed hard from underneath his legs letting out sighs and the weight of the world.

"What's going on man? How's everything?"

"Everything is good brother. I just have a lot on my plate. In about four hours I have to go into the office and have a meeting with the investors for DQS Cosmetics and what really gets me is that with all the money that I have, I still don't have enough to back my line the way the way that it out to be backed up."

Wade shook his head knowingly. He used to work with Dexter when they were first building the business, but he found more comfort in the quiet life with his wife and daughter. He was not built for the ever changing cutthroat world of business but he admired Dexter's ability to handle the pressure.

Dexter went on, I still have to go through all types of red tape and constantly prove myself and my worth to these people that have not only tracked my success over the years but have worked with me. But you know the game Wade. None of that matters. I have to keep proving man."

"Well Dex, I have no doubt that you'll get through this one as well brother. You always do." Dexter smiled. He loved the faith and strength that his family brought. His mother would always hold him on her lap when he cried saying, 'tomorrow is a new day son', and 'it'll be all over in the morning.' He held those beliefs close to him.

"How is the home life man?"

"Ah Wade, nothing like yours. I mean women you know them. You know me…"

Wade smiled. He felt his mother shift in her sleep under his hands. "Look, she's up," he said. Dexter stood and walked over to his mom. "Ma?" Her eyes fluttered. The room was still as Corinne Stiles slowly opened her eyes. The boys held their breath rubbing her hands not wanting to touch her so that she would not fall back in to her sleep. She stared out to no one in particular. Her eyes floated back and forth between the two boys. A barely noticeable smile surfaced on her face. She shut her eyes again. Her face was peaceful, and smooth as a sand dollar.

The boys smiled at each other. Corinne just might make it, especially if she had the love of her two sons with her.

The Fearless Entertainment offices were blaring with music. The bass thumped loudly causing the birds that perched on the windowsill of the of the tenth floor offices to shake as they stared curiously into the windows. Inside a young man was shouting vehemently into his phone. The diamonds that decorated his pinky finger reflecting the light of the sun that shone through the glass as he stood

171

underneath the gold records that bore his name on the placard. Certified Gold, Big City, Fearless Entertainment, "We get busy."

He paced the floors in his white linen suit. His white gators, shined and polished, grazed the pant legs of his suit exposing the gold straps that fastened each shoe. He laughed into the phone flashing a diamond encrusted gold tooth with a dollar sign on it as he spoke. This was a big day for Big City, he had just moved into his new offices and it had only been two weeks, but he was planning to have the party of a lifetime to let everyone know that he was here and ready to do business.

A petite woman with bleached blond hair that gave a sharp contrast to her cinnamon skin walked into the office in a tight blue dress with cup of coffee and scotch in her hand.

She placed it on the desk, dipping as if she were a playboy bunny leaving it on Big City's desk. "Thank you baby," he smiled showing off his dimples.

"We Gets Busy" and other songs from his forthcoming album were in heavy rotation over the loud speaker.

"Check it out," City said. "According to Soundscan my records are in heavy, heavy rotation from here to Atlanta, Miami, California, hell, everywhere. I told you they can't hold me!" he shouted checking his reflection in a mirror on his desk.

"They'll *never* hold me. I'm too large for these boxes they try to put me in. I'll tell anybody, watch your back. The streets are watching and we coming for your position," he said. He laughed to himself, his diamond pendant shaking over his stomach. To any casual onlooker, he was a walking ad for a diamond mine. He sat behind his grand oak desk and smiled.

A life-sized oil painting of himself portrayed as one of the

first presidents smoking a cigar hung on the wall behind him.

"City," the intercom from his desk phone called to him.

"Yeah baby."

"Willie Escobando from Flashy is here to see you," the voice

drawled.

"Ah, yeah. Send him in."

Willie walked into the grand archway of the

picturesque offices that were clearly channeling the Garden of

Eden with its high cherub painted ceilings and oversized

golden doors. The fluorescent lights that lined the walkway

alongside that the small flowing stream that lead to City's

desk made Willie feel like he entered the mind of a rapping

mad hatter. He had met and interviewed a lot of characters

and artists in his day, but there was something different about this one. He had a unique energy and charisma about him. Yet the heavenly décor, mixed in with the questionable women that he hired as "staff" made him all the more of an enigma. Willie quickly tallied up the cost for the million dollar renovations he saw all around him and wondered if he was making all of it from his music.

City definitely fit the profile and the audience of Flashy magazine the only difference was, while a lot of rappers and artists talked about it or rented cars to appear as if they had it, City really did.

"Hey, Mr. City. How are you?" Willie said. He walked in with his usual unassuming presence. His signature red baseball cap and red and white polo button up with jeans always caused him to appear harmless to the artist that he was interviewing. He left himself slightly unshaven which was not

an accident. He knew City was from the Midwest and

probably felt like all New York men had a rugged appearance,

he wanted to maintain that presence.

City rose from behind the desk as Willie entered and

came around to greet him.

"What's up Mr. Escobando, my Puerto Rican brother? How

are you?"

Willie extended his hands and gave Big City a semi-formal

shake.

"Nice watch there," he said admiring the jewelry on Big City's

hands. "I think you're wearing my retirement on your body."

Big City laughed. "What can I say Mr. Escobando. I'm

blessed."

"Clearly you are," Willie said. "Perhaps I need to pray a little harder, you know. But anyway, you got a hot record out right now, the album is about to drop. The new offices here in Midtown and I think I heard whispers about you doing movies. Tell me a little about all that." City smiled taking a sip from his coffee his eyes widening hearing the fruits of his labor told to him.

"Yeah man like I say to everybody, I'm coming for your position. I'm coming for your offices, your building," he said spreading his arms wide as if trying to grip the whole world in them. "Watch out man, I may come for Flashy if it could make me some money." He said with a hint of seriousness in his voice.

"Well, as long as I can stay editor and keep interviewing Flashy and spectacular artists such as yourself, I'm good," Willie laughed.

"Sounds good my man, so what's on the agenda today?" city asked.

"I'm just getting to know you brother. I got the advance copy of the album and it's genius. Rolling stone is saying it's going to go platinum. You already have over a million downloads on the single. How do you feel about that?"

"I feel like it can go diamond, that's how I feel about that. If Shaggy can do it, I can too. I'm just trying to do what I love and be the best."

Big City was serious as he flashed a confident smile and poured more scotch into his coffee. He spoke of his plans for fashion and style and being the biggest style brand in the world for the urban market. What he was most proud of was his new artist that was coming out named Allegria. "She's gorgeous and talented and her music is different and she has international appeal and an international pop sound," he said.

"That's wonderful," Willie said shifting in his seat. "Congrats again."

He took out the folders from his bag and placed them in front of City.

"Let's talk models for the upcoming photo shoot. As you know we are doing the Casino remake. You are going to reprise the Bobby DeNiro character and I wanted to show you a few of the models that we were possibly considering and see what you thought about them." Willie said.

"Before you even show me a picture, make sure in your heart and in your professional opinion that what you are placing before my eyes is a 10 or better. If not, let's postpone the meeting. I don't do average."

"Of course, at Flashy we only hire the best. That's guaranteed."

"I want Tyra," he said.

"Banks?" said Willie.

"Yeah. Or Naomi Campbell."

"Of course I'll look into that." Willie smiled to himself. This kid was outrageous. He could probably get Naomi at the right price if she wanted to do him a favor, but not Tyra. That would be too much work and she didn't need it.

City pressed his intercom and called in his Pamela Anderson look alike that also moonlighted as his secretary. She brought the men refreshers on the drinks.

"So, the best way to get to know me is to live a day in my shoes. You have to live my life and experience this lifestyle to know why it is so great. So I want us to have a few more drinks and then hit the streets. I have a studio session planned a casting and a few other things. I know you wanted to go to my house and we can do that later." City gave him a casual tour of his offices and played him some music all of which Willie found very impressive for such a young man. City's insistence on driving after they both drank so much alcohol in a short amount of time gave him pause, but he really wanted to live the lifestyle as much as possible. He loosened his top button, if Big City's offices and larger than life persona was any indication of how the rest of the day's events were going to go down, he was in for a whirlwind afternoon.

Phoenix fixed her tiny swimsuit in her dressing room at the photo shoot of Wide Open magazine. Her eyes popped with vibrancy as she looked at herself in the mirror. It was amazing what working with the best make-up artists in the industry could do. She never failed to be surprised. In Paris she was a low model on the totem pole and her make-up was often rushed as the other star models were handled with care. Sure she had nice make-up jobs while she worked on her television show but it was such a brief time period. Hell all of it was a flash in the pan. But today she was the star. She was the star of the photo shoot and Joe Malone promised her that it would be worth her effort and time to do this opportunity. Laila sat next to her in the director's chair snacking on the fruit and indulging in the champagne. "Girl, I am so glad that you are back in the N.Y.C. because now I can get all these perks that you are not interested in. Aren't you gonna have a drink? It's free?" she said popping a strawberry in her mouth. Phoenix looked over at Laila. Her eyes looked tired as she chomped hungrily on the goodies. Her blond hair was pulled sloppily into a blond bun strands hung over her bright green jacket and onto her white T-shirt.

"No you go ahead," Phoenix said. "I don't want to get bags under my eyes."

Laila stopped mid bite of her cookie. "Girl all the top models drink, what are you talking about? It's the norm."

"Well, not me. Dexter says that I am ancient."

"Dexter? You quoting him now?" she rolled her eyes. "Girl, he needs to talk less and work more. Word is his position in the industry is on the line. From what I hear Big City is coming up. I love his new song," she danced swinging her hair. "I wonder if he has a girlfriend?"

Phoenix shook her head as she tried to maintain her focus. Laila was just praising Dexter last week and now he was on the way out. Laila fiddled with her phone and snapped a quick selfie, scrunching her nose and making duck lips.

"Girl, I am supposed to have a client meeting this morning. Some basketball player wants me to do his party for him."

"That's good," Phoenix said.

Laila placed her hand on her jeans. "Whatever. He's probably bisexual at most and serial cheater at min, so that's no fun. Hell, I'm looking around at you like I should have stuck with my modeling. Maybe I could have been doing high fashion."

"But look at you now you have your promotions company and you're doing well for yourself, so you don't need the artist gypsy life like I'm living. Look at me. I'm living in a hotel." Phoenix reached for her cell phone it was ringing alerting her of a message received. "I don't want to look at it but it may be my agent," she said glancing at the phone. The phone read a simple *Hello*. That was odd she thought. Who would just send her a message saying hello?

"Who was it?" Laila said. "Your boo Dexter? Damn girl, I still don't know how you got him. Really what's the sex like? He looks crazy. Is he?"

185

"I don't have him Laila. We are simply trying to work together."

"Right right….well he still is interested."

Laila looked at her eyes in the mirror, which reflected the worry that she felt lately. She reached for the brush that sat on the dressing table and brushed her hair back neatly and reapplied her lipstick. Phoenix sat with her eyes closed looking Zen and meditative. Yes, numerically she was twenty-eight years old but she barely looked a day over seventeen, well twenty-one. Her own face looked haggard from years of hard partying. The glow that she had was manufactured and hidden under the bronzer.

She was happy for her friend. She was beautiful and on her way. Lately she had just been feeling like a certain something was missing in her own life.

"I need Botox," she said pushing at the corners of her eyes. A short Asian assistant with black-rimmed glasses stepped into the room. "Hey Phoenix, we need you on set." Phoenix rose to follow her out to the large black platform in the center of a small room. She placed her hands on her hips. Her gold strappy bathing suit hugged her body and showed off her curves. She loved being in front of the camera. It was where she belonged. Joe Malone came over to give her a small pep talk before her shoot and show her a test shot that he had taken.

"See how gorgeous you are," he said holding his camera to her face. "This is going to be fun. Keep it sexy and fun and you should be golden."

Phoenix kissed Joe on the cheek with excitement. She was amazed at how she looked. She could still hang with the

187

young girls in her industry. She knew it was a lot to ask but she hoped that somehow this photo would make the cover. That way Dexter wouldn't worry so much. All she could do was give the shoot all she had. The fan was turned on high as she twisted her body and jutted her hips into seductive poses.

She imagined herself as the temptress seducing the men of America as she blew a kiss to the lens. She had done this many times for Walter but none of it amounted to much. He told her that none of the agencies or clients were interested in her photos because she was over twenty-one.

"That's right momma, keep it sexy," Laila yelled from the wings.

Laila looked on at Phoenix, the girl was working it. She felt a tinge of sadness when she saw Phoenix out there bouncing around. She wondered if she would have had what it took to

188

be a top model. She definitely had the height and the body for it. But too many of life's circumstances kept getting in the way, like her relationship with Jacob.

She had been putting so much focus on their relationship, she had forgotten about some personal meetings that she had set up and hadn't been as aggressive about going after clients. Phoenix walked off the platform over to Laila. "So how did I look?"

"You looked hot, you were working it," she said. "Do you want to go and get some lunch after this?

"Actually, I need to go and meet Dexter. He wants to talk to me about the campaign I guess. So I am going to hurry and pack up my things."

Laila kissed her cheek. "Ok honey. Congrats again. You looked great. Call me."

Phoenix waved her goodbye and stepped into her dressing room door.

"What in the world is this?" she said her eyes looking at the three dozen yellow roses on her dressing table. "Who did this?" she looked around. The room smelled of a rose garden as she walked over excitedly to see who they were from. "No card."

"That's strange. Could it be Dexter?"

Phoenix walked down the hall to find Arthur, Joe's Assistant, to ask if he knew who may have sent the roses."

"I'm not sure Phoenix. I didn't see anyone come through here. But honey, you know how men are, they love sending the models flowers as a gift of appreciation of the fantasy. Just take them home and forget about it."

"You're right. You have a good night."

190

Phoenix walked back to her dressing room walking past the next model that was scheduled with Joe. She couldn't have been more than 19. Phoenix sucked in and smiled. She watched as the girl trotted on stage with a wide eyed wide empty expression as she adjusted the globe sized breasts that were spilling out of her top.

"Dear God," Phoenix sighed walking into her dressing room. She stared at her face in the mirror. "Maybe I am ancient," she said to herself. She threw on jeans a white T-shirt, black cowboy boots and headed out the door to Soho. All of a sudden she had a desperate need to be next to Dexter and it was not about business. Dexter had been leaving her messages since early this morning saying that they needed to meet. They hadn't seen each other since he pushed her out of the car and was slightly apprehensive.

She hadn't wanted things to end that way between them especially since for a moment they seemed to have a connection. She didn't think her life would be such a sensitive area for Dexter. His eyes seemed to plead to her to be on his side. Maybe she would be able to smooth things over a little better once she got to lunch. She grabbed a rose and put it in her bag as a surprise.

Chapter Seven

Laila stubbed out her joint as she pulled in front of her brownstone. The champagne had already made her a little tipsy and she was feeling lightheaded from the marijuana. She told herself she wasn't going to smoke anymore but after checking her bank account earlier she realized that she had to escape the stress she felt. She had given a large part of her savings to Jacob so that he could get out of debt and start his business.

She had given him $30,000 it was almost all that she had. He was supposed to be making payments, but his business was going slow and he hadn't been able to pay it back. In addition, the money had been causing tension between them and she wanted it to end. She offered Jacob to stay with her and so they could combine their efforts. Jacob wasn't too keen on the idea, especially coming from living with someone already for eight years.

He wanted his own space and to figure things out. She got out of her Range Rover and walked into her house. The dishes piled the sink. The counters were flooded with empty champagne and wine bottles, and cigarette butts were stubbed out in various coffee mugs baring red lipstick rings all around her house.

She threw her bag on the couch and went upstairs into her office and tried to do some work. She had been hitting the club circuit pretty hard this week in attempts to garner new clients and build some business relationships but it seemed that she was merely chasing Jacob around from club to club trying to keep tabs on him and make him notice her. It was really affecting her business the overdue bills were beginning to pile up on her bureau. Maybe she needed to hire an intern. She just didn't have the energy to keep up with everything lately. She flayed her head down on the desk feeling it swirl in a calming fog as all worry escaped her mind. Her eyes watered thinking about the $1100 dollar mortgage that was due again. She may need to refinance her home. *Bills, Bills, Bills!* She banged her hands on her desk.

How did Phoenix do it? She always seemed to be able to just jump in with two feet without trying and bounce back. She was able to attract everything to her effortlessly. Did she need to read The Secret? It was not fair.

Laila reached down into her file cabinet and pulled out her old modeling photos. "Damn, I was sexy. I wish I would have known that," she said. "But what I can do is make money. Not everyone can do that!" She tossed her pictures on the ground and pulled up her calendar. Big City was having a party in a couple of weeks and she needed to get a piece of that action. Maybe she could recoup the money Jacob blew up his nose or on another woman. It was certainly not on a business venture. Money was becoming tight and she needed all the help she could get. The real question was how could should meet a fine brother like Dexter, get in good, and get some help. If Phoenix could do it, she surely could too. She would just have to figure out how. She picked up the phone and put in a call to Big City's assistant. She needed to get into that party tonight.

Phoenix walked over to the patio chair, rose in hand, where Dexter sat talking on the phone. He looked casual in a peach polo and tan shorts. His skin glistened with health and leisure as he sipped on a Bellini. He rose from his chair to give Phoenix a kiss as she came over. "Wow, a rose for me? How romantic. I thought that was supposed to be my job." Phoenix looked at him quizzically. Perhaps the roses weren't from him.

"Consider them a peace offering," she said. "From me to you." She was taken aback at how good he looked today. His smile broadened when he saw her taking her hands in his and kissing them. "You look stunning," he said not taking his eyes off of her. "Thank you. I just came back from a photo shoot. How are you? You look great."

"I'm well. I met with Roger Steinberg at Revlon briefly regarding the product and I showed them your picture and it looks as if they are excited about meeting you."

"What do you mean?"

"I mean that I want you to be my model. I want you to be the face of the DQS Cosmetics campaign." He reached out and grabbed her hand so that she would make no mistake that he was talking to her directly.

 "I think that you're gorgeous and the natural beauty that I have been looking for. The decision is up to me, and I choose you."

Phoenix sat in her seat stunned at the news. She felt her feet grow numb and tingly. She was not expecting to hear this. She ran her fingers through her hair placing the stray locks behind her ears, smiling. She was more than surprised she was elated. She burst into laughter. "Are you serious Dexter?" "Yes," he said laughing, pausing only to emphasis his seriousness by looking deep into her eyes. "I am dead serious." The laughter stopped as he stared at her. He seemed to be serious about more than one thing. He knew without a doubt that he wanted her for the face of this campaign. "Thank you Dexter, thank you so much. I don't know what to say?" she said reaching over and kissing his cheek.

"No thank you. The shots you took are beautiful you deserve to be up on the billboards with your name up in lights. Little girls will reverie your beauty. Men will want their wives to look like you. It's my pleasure and my honor to work with you from the ground up."

The waiter came over to check on the table. Dexter ordered a mimosa for Phoenix.

"Dexter it's the middle of the day," she said.

"I know but it's a special occasion and this place makes the best Mimosa's. I want to celebrate with you, that's why I invited you to come here. Then we're off to dinner."

"*Dinner?* Dex-"

He put his hand to her mouth, "Please let me take you to dinner. I want to show my new star model a good time."

Phoenix exhaled into submission. What else could she do? She felt like a princess at the ball and this could not have come at a better time. The photo shoot and now the campaign—this day was turning out to be amazing, she sipped her mimosa feeling victorious. Dexter brought out plans for the billboards and marketing schedules that Phoenix would be involved in over the course of the year. It was a one-year contract for $150,000 that would become negotiable after the second year if all went well.

"So enough about work," Dexter said. "Excuse me for a moment he said reaching for his phone. "Have the car pull up to the front I want to make sure that we have enough time to make that flight.

Dexter hung up the phone and reached his hand out to her.

"Come on sweetheart let's go."

"Go where?"

"I told you that we were going to dinner right?

"Yes?"

"Well come on," he said grabbing her hand.

The black SUV rolled over and the two got in and began to ride through the city. Dexter pulled her closer. Phoenix looked at the Billboards as they rode through Times Square imagining her face on the Billboards. This was going to be major. She closed her eyes and pressed her face against the window. Feeling light-headed she drifted off into a subtle daydream.

"Walter," Phoenix said. "I'm leaving you."

Walter rose from the stool he sat on in his studio. His eyes were vacant as he focused in on the photographs from his most recent photo shoot.

"What are you talking about your leaving me? Where are you going to go?"

"I am going to Paris."

"Paris? Why? Because you did two successful shoots that I got for you and now you are leaving me to go to Paris?" he never averted his eyes

from his portraits. His body thin and frail as he placed the photos side by side.

"The shoot that I shot with this new model Gabrielle was amazing. I think that Vogue may want this one. I was testing her out to see if possibly I could submit some photos to the editorial department for consideration. This could really be the shot that we've been waiting on Phe. I just need you to believe in me a little bit longer." He said tossing the photos to the side and rising from his stool. Phoenix stood frozen in fear, but felt bold as a lion. She gripped her small bags in her hands.

"I know, I have heard all of this before Walter, but I have to go and do my own thing now."

"I gave you everything I had," he said gripping her wrists. "Look at this bracelet, look at your ears with diamonds huh? It's me, all of it." He threw her wrist down as he walked over to the window.

"Fuck Phoenix! I love you. Doesn't that mean anything to you anymore or are you so hell bent on getting to the top that you can just cast me aside and cast our love aside in order to get to where you need to go."

"I am not casting you aside Walter. Look at you. Your thin, your sick."

"And you'd leave me like this?"

"You're overworked and you just can't keep your promises."

"I fell on hard times Phoenix can I get any slack here? I'm trying."

"Just like you tried to get a divorce from the wife you hid from me for four years."

Walter stood still his old shoulders shaking. He wanted to pull himself away from the window but he stood there with his arms folded across his chest. Sometimes in life things don't always go as planned. His dreams were big and vast and Phoenix was his goose that laid the golden eggs. He had known that one day this moment would come. He tried to prolong it as long as he could. He tried to keep her from the prying hands of the world and give her all that she needed. In the beginning she didn't need much. She needed his comfort as much as he needed her innocence. It was an equal exchange of companionship. He turned from the window to face her. Her face was hard as concrete. Prior to this moment he had not been given the ability to see her as she was.

"Where are you going to go out there in the big wide world?" he said voice retreating.

"I am going to Paris."

"Paris! How are you going to afford that?"

"I don't know and I don't care."

He walked over to her reaching for her arms that stiffened at his touch. His hands trembled as he released her, feeling the life energy drain from her with his grip. Saddened he stepped back rubbing the pain that had risen in his temples.

"I left the key in the Bible next to the bed. Good luck Walter."

"Phoenix? Phoenix? Are you ok? You seem literally a million miles away right now on presumably the best day of your life." Phoenix's eyes began to sting as she fought back the tears that were fighting to forge their way down her face. She let out a small cough hoping to force them back in. She pulled her face away from the glass and looked at Dexter who gave her a wink.

"I'm overjoyed. I can't even believe I am here."

"That's what I like to hear. I thought you were sleep or something, you went away from me for a minute."

"No, never."

206

"Good," he said. "I want to keep you close. We have a lot of magic to make together."

She moved in closer to him trying to fit herself under his arm. She sensed his protection and put her arm around his waist. She wanted to mesh herself into him if not forever, for just a moment. She felt safe in his arms and in his presence like a princess in an ivory tower.

She silently prayed to God thanking him for the contract. Maybe her face would be put so high up on the billboards and her name so big up in lights that her past could no longer reach her. Walter could no longer find her, she could no longer find her, and the fiery sting of shadows past could no longer overtake her. She just wanted to plant her feet on stable ground somehow.

Dexter lifted her chin to look her in the eyes.

"You sure you're alright?"

"Yeah, I guess I'm just a little overwhelmed."

"Well, it only gets better," he said.

"What now Dexter?"

"We are going to have to pack up your hotel room so that you can live like a civilized person."

"What are you talking about Dexter?"

"I have a spot I got for you to stay at on Madison Ave. It's gorgeous you'll love it. It's close to work and the DQS offices. It has a great view and you don't have to worry about anything, except moving in and getting some rest and getting out of that hotel. Soho Grand is nice, but it's nothing like having your own place."

Wow, she thought, he was taking care of everything. It was all moving so fast. They pulled up to a huge house outside of the city

that Phoenix had never seen before. The pair rolled on in
silence. Dexter reached into his pocket and produced a black
sash.

"What is that for?" she said.

"This is for your eyes he said turning her around placing it
over her eyes.

"Why are you blindfolding me?" she said removing the sash
from her eyes.

"What? You don't trust me?" he said.

"Yeah, I trust you. I just want to know what's going on."

"Well that's not trust is it if your questioning me."

He turned her around slowly putting the blindfold on her.
He kissed her neck gently as he led her out of the car. The
walk was long as Phoenix fumbled along blindly over grass,
gravel, and then concrete.

"We're almost there," Dexter said. Her body trembled with anticipation. As she stepped along further she felt the air grow hot as she heard the sounds of a loud engine roaring with a high pitch sound.

"Don't let go," Dexter said squeezing her hand tighter.

He led her up a narrow flight of steps and sat her down. The carpet felt thick under her boots. The leather squished beneath her on the couch.

"Ok Dexter, where are we."

Dexter pulled off her blindfold. Phoenix gasped she was on a plane.

"What is this?" she said.

"It's my jet. It's nothing much, just a G4 for now, but I'm proud of it."

She rose from the couch. Her mouth so wide flies could have flown in.

Phoenix scanned the details of the room and stared at the white leather seats trimmed in gold. Her eyes roamed over the flat screen TV that hung neatly in the wooden panel over the credenza. She walked past for the four chairs in the main seating area to the large wooden door that opened to the bedroom equipped with a queen sized bed. She kicked off her boots and laid back on the white bed spread with the gold letter DQS imprinted on the front.

Dexter came into the room and sat next to her.

"So what do you think?"

"I think that, God must have thought a whole lot about me to bring me here."

"Well, I would have to agree with God. I think a whole lot about you too and that is why I brought you here. I hope that you can see yourself getting used to traveling like this." Phoenix sat up and throwing her hands in the air as if she were a ten year old girl sliding down a slide for the first time. "Are you kidding me? Of course I could see myself flying like this? What woman couldn't? Dexter, this is so beyond anything that I could have ever imagined," she said. "I'm just a girl from Detroit; my parents were hardworking middle class people. My dad worked at Ford and my mom was a nurse. I-I-don't really know what to say right now. I think I just want to lie back down."

Dexter smiled as he stroked her leg.

"You can do whatever you want. You haven't officially started work yet and signed your contracts so you still have a little time to relax and enjoy life for the moment."

"Wait," she said propping herself up on one arm. "Where exactly are we flying to?"

"Well, I wanted to show you a few markets that I was considering having Billboards posted and I wanted to steal you away for an evening so that you could get a nice meal and relax with one of the best chef's in LA."

"LA?"

"Yes, we are going to Malibu to be exact. Ever since I was a little kid and I used to watch movies and stuff, I used to fantasize about being an actor like Sydney Poitier or Denzel Washington. Obviously I am no actor but I stayed in a house in Malibu for my first Grammy's and ten years later I got something of my own." Her face beamed up at him, with a light that was blinding because the source was purely from her heart.

She put her hands on his shoulders and whispered in his ear. "Perhaps one day, after I am making millions modeling and acting you can come and fly on my plane."

"Yeah," he said. "Anything can be achieved through hard work. You just need someone to help get you to that next level. That's what I had, someone who believed in me."

"Like you believe in me?"

"Yeah, like I believe in you."

Time stopped as they stared at each other sealing an unspoken fate in their eyes.

At this moment so much was being said and yet not a word was exchanged.

He wanted to know where this woman came from; appearing in his life so unexpectedly. She was a stranger, but for whatever reason there was an inexplicable tug that kept him wanting to see her. Perhaps it was her body, smooth and creamy as a tall cup of café au lait. Maybe was it her hair that she wore as a crown of glory thick and full slightly past her shoulders. Was it her skin, which was often devoid of make-up showing its perfection in structure and even her blemishes, which seemed to exist separately from her face reminding him that she indeed was human. Or was it those eyes? Those doe-like brown angelic eyes that had a voice all their own. He settled on her smile. She was so open and honest. From the moment she looked at him out on the terrace of The Lounge, she was always forcing him to be honest. It was a good feeling, refreshing.

"So, why don't you give me the number to your room at the Soho Grand and I will have someone pack up the room and get the stuff over to Madison Ave and it will be there by the morning."

"Dexter," she said. "I don't know if I want you to do all of that."

"What's the problem? You're living in a hotel it's time to get your own place and here it is. I'm sure your intentions weren't to come to New York and live in a hotel."

"I know but within the last three hours my whole life has changed."

"Phoenix I asked you to move, not get married. Welcome to the fast lane. You've got to think quick on your feet."

"Dexter-"

"What's the number Phoenix?" Dexter said.

"Dexter listen-"

"The number, I asked one question."

Phoenix put her hands over her eyes. Her life seemed to be flashing before them at lighting speed as if she were being rushed through the airport to catch a flight. Yes, her dreams were at her feet, but she didn't think that they would be here this soon or perhaps in this way.

Dexter stood up from the bed.

"Maybe I was wrong about you; maybe you aren't ready for the magnitude of this position. A top model must be ready at all times, and clearly you're not. So before you try and fly me around in anything and get to where I am you need to learn to be ready."

He walked out of the room leaving a stunned Phoenix, her heart racing in fear, lying on the bed. She could hear him in the other room placing phone calls. Dexter was right. She just thought of packing her room herself and moving in to the new home of her choice with her own money, not something that Dexter had picked out for her without her consent. She walked into the room where he was. She looked around the cabin, she did want this. She couldn't have dreamed it with her own eyes. She felt like a giant walking amongst the crowd when she was with Dexter and there was no way she could let that go. She allowed desperation and desire to pull her out into the main cabin where Dexter sat.

"212-487-7987," she said head facing south arms hugging her shoulders.

"What are you talking about?"

"212-487-7987. That's the number to the hotel. Room 428.

He looked at her in silence.

"You better sit down, we'll be landing soon."

Dexter knew that she would see things his way, but what she didn't know is that he had already called ahead and had her things packed up anyway.

The jet touched down in Malibu. The ocean was clear blue as the surfers caught the waves that came crashing into the shoreline. The beach bums and bunnies lounged around in the sand. Joggers jogged past the rollerbladers that laughed and held hands. Phoenix noticed all of these things from the Mercedes they rode in as they sped along the PCH towards Dexter's house. She hadn't been to California in a long time, and had forgotten the smell of the ocean and they casualness of the atmosphere. Here Phoenix felt as though she could just kick her feet up.

They rode for nearly forty-five minutes down the PCH delighting in the fresh smell of salt water rising off the ocean. As they raced towards Zuma Beach, The car pulled up to a silver metallic set of door surrounded by windows. At first glance the house appeared to be a small cottage but as the two stepped in Phoenix saw that the house expanded more than 10,000 square feet. She could look straight from the front door to the patio and grass area in the back that over looked the ocean.

A golden Labrador came running and barking to the front door.

Dexter bent down giving him a rough pat.

"What's up Russell," he said. "I named him after Russell Simmons." Dexter went into the kitchen to grab a water.

"You want some?"

"Sure," she said reaching for the water. "Who lives here, if you live in New York?"

"Well, this actually is the place that Lisa and I bought together because so much of our life brought us out this way and still does, so we wanted to be comfortable."

"So this is her house?"

"No, this is going to be my house and I am giving her the apartment on the Upper West Side since she spends most of her time there. She has a house in Georgia near her family and I am sure that is where she is going to want to spend the majority of her time."

Phoenix didn't want to go near that subject. She felt a small pang of jealousy as she thought of Dexter and Lisa purchasing property together. But she wasn't going to let her mind wander over to matters that had nothing to do with her plans. And that was making a name for herself. It was all she felt she truly had.

Dexter stroked Phoenix's arm.

"Listen, she wanted to have something to contribute, but if it makes you feel any better I put down the down payment. Anyway, I was thinking about moving my mom up here once she got out of the hospital or maybe just take her out of the hospital and bring her here near the water where she can have peace and 24-hour care."

"What's wrong with your mother?"

"She has cancer. And it's bad, very, very bad. Stage four."

"I'm sorry," Phoenix said.

"Yeah," he scratched his neck moving away from her.

"Where is Rosanda?" he said calling the housekeeper's name as he went from room to room.

The small cocoa colored woman came from outside the house into the kitchen swatting Dexter on the behind.

"Ju no yell at me Meeester Deyxter Stiles! Ju no better den dat," Rosanda said. He was used to her thick Puerto Rican accent reprimanding him. "Ju no call Ms. Rosanda telling me ju coming or not. I no having anything made for ju and jur freynds right now."

"I'm sorry Rosanda," he said bending down to give her a kiss on the cheek. The two laughed playfully. "Ju no I don't like that."

"I know, I know. I'm sorry."

"Where is Ms. Lisa, she coming today?"

"No, no Lisa is not coming today. But, I want you to meet Phoenix Mitchell. She is a friend of mine and my new model."

"Okay, nice to meet you," she said nodding politely. Her eyes quickly looked Phoenix up and down. Dexter was like a son and she was very protective of him. She was never too fond of him bringing new models to the house. She was always skeptical of their intentions. This one seemed to be okay, but she wasn't sure. Dexter noticed the old woman lingering a little too long on the handshake and separated the two.

"Hey Rosanda, we are going to go out in the pool and relax. Could you make up some dinner for us?

"Sure."

He leaned down to her ear to whisper a few more instructions

"Thanks, Rosanda."

There was nothing like swimming in the pool overlooking the ocean.

"So what do you think of everything so far."

"I think the way that you live is amazing."

He smiled sheepishly.

"There are bathing suits in the bathroom on the right side of the living room."

Phoenix walked past the suspicious Rosanda who watched after her as she walked down the hall. The ocean breeze blew through the windows as she went into the bathroom.

"Swimsuits all ready huh? I wonder whose these are. Lisa's?"

She grabbed the blue one piece that had side slits to show off her physique. The bra cups squeezed in on her breasts forcing them upward toward her chin. She walked out back to Dexter who was sitting in boxer briefs, looking out onto the water. The air was so still as if the winds were waiting too massage anyone that came into its gentle embrace into a deep sleep.

Phoenix walked over and sat next to Dexter. Both facing the water. Both taking in the breeze. They sat in silence oblivious to time and the world around them. The two talked endlessly as if from a continuation of previous conversation that was started a long time ago.

"This place is beautiful," Phoenix said.

"Yeah, I wish that I could get back here more often," Dexter said his cell phone falling to the concrete beneath him. "Maybe one day. I look around sometimes and all this shit seems like maintenance." His brow furrowed as he sat up in his seat not looking at Phoenix. Phoenix walked next to him and rubbed his back. "I got all the money in the world and I still can't make my mom well. I got all the money in the world and I still can't find the time to see her. I got all I could ever think of and I can only be in one house at a time."

Phoenix reached up to rub his back. Her hand was met with a back stiffened from the touch of true affection.

"I got everything, but sometimes, it feel like I ain't got shit, but maintenance."

There was no way in. His words had a finality that hung in the air as he spoke them. Phoenix wanted to remind him of the times that he was kid on the block in Bedstuy and how far he had made it, but her futile attempts were interrupted by the shrill sound of Rosanda calling them in to dinner.

The smell of lamb and salad discoed through the room seducing the pair out of their seats. Phoenix felt like a princess as she sat at the wooden table across from Dexter as they looked out onto the ocean. "This is so surreal right now," she said.

"What?"

"This. All of this. This is not real. It's like a dream. It just feels like it's not going to last forever. Like it can't last forever," she looked down at her plate.

"It can last as long as you want. I mean don't think like that. You're here aren't you?" "Right," she breathed. "I am." Phoenix felt this could not last forever and would not last forever. This was the thing of dreams. And this was just one summer.

He poured her Pellegrino and cut up her lamb. She licked her fork and clicked her teeth with the cold metal made warm by the moisture of her lips. He smiled and dabbed the corners of her mouth, she giggled and traced a small outline of his mouth with her fingertips. He put them in his mouth.

Her fingers waited awhile, and tapped at his tongue. He

rinsed her flavor with fizzy lemon lime zest from his glass. He

said it went down like sweet ambrosia. Her heart began to

leap with fear as they got up from the table. She wondered

where this was all going. He said he had known all along.

Her nipples jumped when he touched them. She was unsure

of what was resting in her panties. His fingers went to find

out. The journey was smooth her caramel skin slick and her

breathing shallow. She opened her eyes, not remembering

how she got into the bedroom. They smiled at each other

laughing at their secret joke.

He looked at her as if it was his first time and she

looked at him as if it were hers. It was the first time; the first

time for this. Her breasts ached with longing as he pulled

down her bathing suit top. They were swollen and ripe like the skin of two melons and the juice was equally as sweet. His kisses felt like fire and Phoenix let out a whimper. She knew now why girls called grown men daddy because her body had been resurrected with each kiss. He removed his white t-shirt. The cool of the fabric brushed across her face in his hurriedness. She drank it in, because it smelled of him. His chest was heavy on her body and she didn't mind the weight. It felt so good to be crushed. It felt so good to be bent. Her legs spread for him as if upon silent command. This was the first time they had been truly opened. He spread them wider with his thighs. Her heartbeat had left her chest and wandered down between the smooth surfaces between her legs. His mind's eye only saw what was before him.

As he moved deeply and rhythmically inside of her he tried to be gentle. He kissed her forehead. His last intention was to hurt her. He had hurt enough people in his life and he wanted to make this one right. Her face winced as he entered her. Yet the look in her eyes said, "I'm still here" as she met him half way. Their eyes never left each other. The room was so silent, but inside them was so loud, hard, slow, and fast. They were dancing to all the R&B, hip Hop reggae, and jungle beats that pulsed between them. He kissed her tears and there were many. She stroked his back and he needed it.

His breath was hard and deep. It came from his belly. It came from a hunger. It was primal when he came. She was feline when she came. And they were so happy that they had come together. They stayed in each other's grasp when they were done. Their faces were smooth, slack jawed and

231

unsmiling. This is what their nakedness looked like. They stared at the ceiling and held onto each other for dear life. He with her hand on his back; and her lying gently under his arm.

Chapter Eight

Willie gripped the brim of his baseball cap as Big City sped and pushed his car like a crazed fanatic through the streets of New York. "You know I love living in New York City. It's the best city in the world. I love being a part of the action. It's amazing." "I do think that America sleeps on the Mid- West so I had to come and show them how we do it. For culture and for history," City said taking a sharp turn. "There are millions and millions of unclaimed dollars in this world and I am trying to get my hands on as much as I can grip in my fists," he laughed punching the air.

They winded up 125th street where City pointed out to Willie a restaurant that he was planning to open up for his

sister to run. "See I have a big family. I have a lot of people to help. I have a lot of people on my team. I want to put a real soul food and rib joint over on this block. Maybe Bill Clinton will come and have some wings or something."
"Well this is something that we definitely want to see in Flashy magazine."

The two pulled into the Heartland studios located in the heart of Harlem. They were met by a parade of girls for the casting of Big City's new video for the song, Five Finger Discount." The castings offices smelled of lust and greed as they walked in. Girls that had seen and known city inadvertently through his shows flocked to his sides when he entered. He dealt with each woman casually and with ease as if he were her best friend. He obviously loved women and loved the attention. It was obvious that they loved him too.

His swagger was part street and part lion as he maneuvered through the room.

His platinum chain swinging as a young pretty woman, obviously an assistant ran over to him and brought him a drink.

The two entered the casting session already taking place and watched as the aspiring video vixens showed their dancing skills on the pole located in the middle of the room. Willie watched in earnest as the mini strip show went on before his eyes and one after another the girls came and gave City a kiss on the cheek as if he were a King.

"So, is this the kind of lady that you want us to show on your arm? I think we were right about the whole Casino theme for the magazine its perfect."

"Nope, that one is for the bedroom. I don't want anyone on my arm."

City was tireless as he watched girl after girl dance and twirl for several hours. His eyes focused in with precision. When City felt thoroughly satisfied he wanted to head to the studio and lay more tracks for the album.

"All of a sudden, I feel inspired so let's go," he said sipping some green tea mixed with Hennessey. Willie was starting to feel a bit nauseous from all the drinking. "Hey City is there a secret amphetamine I don't know about? We have been at it for hours," Willie said.

City shot him a look. "Don't be weak Escobando. We're high on life and green tea right now. Reach into your inner power. Haven't you ever read Deepak Chopra? C'mon man let's work." City marched out of his truck with Willie

236

stumbling behind him. They walked into the IT Factory to work. The faces of the great artists lined the walls. City looked on expectant that soon his photo would be on the wall as well. Willie liked his style. He was flashy and given to obvious indulgence but he had a passion and a drive for success and the finer things in life, and surprisingly he was health nut of sorts. Minus all the drinking. He pulled out his pad to jot down a few quick notes about what he had seen in the studio.

"So City, you have a lot to be proud of right now brother, you have the new offices on 5th Ave, the magazine spread in flashy devoted to you, the hot new video that's about to drop and the major party that is about to pop off in the Hamptons. How did a relatively unknown brother like you come up from obscurity over the last year and a half and become a power house."

"Well, first of all let me start by saying that the streets are always watching. I've been a patient and quiet observer of this game for a long time, and I always had it in the back if my mind what I wanted to do and what I was going to do. So this isn't new to me."

"True that. I know a lot of hardworking artists that are still trying to get the notoriety that you have. They have been at it for years and they didn't become so respected and revered in such a short amount of time. How did you manage that?"

"Hard work and God. That's it."

"Well I know that you got your first start about four years back from Dexter Stiles, now there are rumors circulating of a beef, how do you feel about that?"

"Well I'll say it's a lot of jealousy in the industry. People want you to do things their way and advance at their pace. That's unfortunate. It's true Dexter introduced me around, but he was mismanaging the opportunities that were coming my way, and blocking my money out of jealousy. You know every dynasty has its fall and now it's time for his."

"Well, you know that with so much violence and beefs in the industry don't you think that it's your responsibility to help support other people like yourself to be more positive and everyone grow and nation build?"

"That's all well and good, but I am from the streets. Dexter is from the streets. A lot of people are from the streets and there are some things that are just not done. Just print this, I project a billion dollars in my future and I won't let anyone stand in the way of that. This party that I want to have the magazine be a part of is going to be epic. I want you to have a

front row seat. That's all you need to print. Epic. Epic. Epic.

Ya dig?"

Phoenix rolled over in her sleep. The sun peered

through the window signaling the early morning. She may

have been dreaming but it sounded as if hummingbirds

serenaded the pair in the bed. Dexter rolled over smiling, a

gentle grin on his face. He leaned over kissing Phoenix his

toothy grin giving way to coolness. Phoenix smiled. She

stared up at the ceiling wondering if she had dreamt the

whole scene lastnight. It was the soreness of her body that let

her know everything was real. Dexter picked up his phone

that had been ringing incessantly since the wee hours of the morning.

He flung off the white bed sheets and headed toward the bathroom.

"We have to get shaking. I have to get back to New York and you start work at the end of the week. I want you to go through some treatments in preparation for the campaign and then there are some meetings…"his voice trailed off as he looked at Phoenix on the bed.

He came back and sat next to her on the end of the bed and rubbed her hair.

"You are truly beautiful," he said. "Inside and well, out."

Phoenix smiled as he walked back into the shower. She looked over at her cellphone, it was June 6th. She made a

241

mental note in her brain to meet up with Willie and Big City tomorrow. She had to get back to New York. All of this seemed like a dream, but if everything went according to plan she would not only be the star of DQS Cosmetics but also a promising leading model and actress. She fell back on the bed feeling satisfied with herself. Her lips were still hot with love from the night before. Perhaps being with Dexter wasn't a good move. She didn't want to mix business and pleasure but it was hard to deny her growing feelings for him. Dexter had almost said that he loved her lastnight, but stopped himself.

Phoenix wasn't sure if she was ready for love, but she was ready to see her name in lights and Dexter was more than willing and able to see her get there. Her cellphone vibrated on the bed beside. She picked up the phone in hesitation of the blocked ID number.

"Hello?" she said. The phone was dead silent on the end.

"Hello?" Phoenix spoke again looking up at the phone as if would answer her back.

She hung up the phone. "That's strange."

Dexter came out of the shower naked. His body glistened with beads of water. He smiled as he stood confidently staring at her, showing off his athletic build.

"You going to shower? We have to be in NY by 9."

Phoenix rose from the bed dropping her nightie and displaying her supple build as well. They seemed to have changed, both glowing and youthful. They were ignited like kindred spirits tapped into the inexplicable fountain of youth. Phoenix playfully dodged Dexter's embrace as she charted off into the shower smiling.

The shower felt warm and the bathroom felt safe. Wherever she was with Dexter she felt safe. As she lathered her body she couldn't help but feel a small pang of fear that ran through her. She knew Dexter's feelings on her pictorial in Flashy magazine and more importantly she knew Dexter's feelings on Big City. She wanted to do that spread, not to make City's empire grow but for herself. She prayed to God silently hoping that Dexter would understand. Phoenix knew that she would be risking her own contract with DQS Cosmetics to have a side hustle on her own, but it was something that she had to do for herself. If everything went according to how she saw it in her mind, she soon would be an even bigger name than DQS Cosmetics or the urban market alone could have ever imagined. She was the quintessential hybrid that was missing she decided.

Chapter Nine

The sun shone bright over Brooklyn. Laila and Jacob sat staring lovingly at each other. His dark blue knit polo hugging every muscle on his back. Laila could barely keep herself from grinning. She understood at that very moment why she loved him. His white teeth beamed at her as he spoke, lips pink and dewy with moisture. They were a sharp contrast to dark coal hues of his skin. Jacob was a cool drink of water and Laila found herself thirsty every time she saw him. The restaurant was new and nestled deep in the enclaves of Park Slope that sat off to the side at a corner table in the back of the restaurant sipping wine and playing hooky. Jacob went on about his plans to open up his own gym and Laila listened on intently, leaning forward with every word hoping that the deep slit in the front her dress was revealing enough cleavage in order to entice Jacob into staying the night with her. She sipped her wine and rubbed the glass in a circle making a slight humming noise as she swirled it around. He didn't seem to notice as he went on eating his fish and rattling off his list nutrition supplements that he was currently taking. "I know a better supplement you can have. It's100% healthy, won't make you gain weight. As a matter of fact, I promise it will cause you to lose a pound or two." She took a seductive sip of her wine and peered over the glass.

"Sounds good, I may have to try that out."

"Well, if you have time, you can try it out now. Why wait?"

Laila giggled seductively.

Jacob dropped his fork on the plate causing it to clink in aggravation.

"Were you listening to me at all? I'm telling you some pretty major stuff right now and thought you may have been interested, but I guess not."

"I am interested," she said coyly." I am interested in you."

"See, that's what I mean Laila, your mind is never on business. It's always on my dick, or the club, or parties."

"That's not true."

"It is. When was the last time Lady J promotions put on something major?"

Laila blinked her eyes, attempting to put into to focus the man that had been recently turned into a monster.

"I haven't seen or heard from you in over a week, I just wanted to keep the conversation light and focus on us."

"Me opening up my gym *is* me. I thought you were supportive," he said.

"I am supportive Jacob. I think the $30,000 which made up my life savings was my way of showing support."

"Awww, here we go. You throwing that shit in my face. Look, your little money is on the way, so don't start. A woman is supposed to help her man."

"And a man is not supposed to disappear for weeks and days at a time."

"Look Laila, you knew what was up going into this. I told you, I am in a complicated situation that I am trying to get out of. Some days are better than others. Most days, I'm just trying to keep the peace."

"Jacob, you can stay with me. I told you that. Come rest your head, please, let me help you," she said reaching for his hand.

Jacob pushed his plate from in front of upsetting the red wine onto the white tablecloth.

"Damn you sound like my wife! You don't get it baby do you? I'm a man. I have to do this on my own."

Laila put her head down, preparing herself for the gush of tears that were threatening to flood her lap.

"Your *wife?*

"I'm trying to be with you. Don't you see that? I'm trying to give you all of me. Don't you see that?"

She fanned her face, now red and looked into Jacob's eyes that pleaded with her to believe him. How could she not? This was the only man that had professed his desire in life to make her happy. This was the man, that wanted to abstain from sex because he felt her too delicate. This was the man that had wined and dined her all over New York City when they first met and protected her from the swarm of men that tried to take advantage of her. He was her Knight in Shining Armor, so she thought. Lately all they did was fight over time and space and the limited supply of both. Laila had been so confused lately, especially since she had given him the money to jumpstart his business that never materialized. He always seemed angry and distant when she asked questions about it. Now he finally said it.

"When were you going to tell me about her?"

"Come on Laila. You're not a child. You knew what was up. This is rough on me as it is. I'm trying to make my decisions and what for? You don't care about me. I might as well stay where I am."

Laila's head was spinning.

"Jacob, look, I don't want to fight with you. I am sorry if I wasn't listening to your plans for a gym. I do care and I do think they are important."

"Good because I need your support right now. I may need another $5,000 to get things really going. I've spent that on you with these dinners basically. We'd be even," he said biting into his fish.

Laila trembled. All she ever wanted was love. But she would have to get to that later. She didn't know if Jacob was foreal or trying to hurt her. He was being so casual about everything. If it was true, why was he here?

"Well, I would like your support too, if possible."

"With what?" he said not looking up.

"I know you hate big parties and events, but I was hoping that you would make an exception. I am pretty sure that I will be one of the promoters invited to work on Big City's album release party next month and I would really like it if you could be there with me. It gets lonely not having my man with me by my side at these events."

"I'm sure you have your friends and the people at the party."

"What is it with you? I already told you Laila, I'm not feeling the whole going out to the club scene in New York."

"This is not just the going out scene. This is my work."

"Well, I'll see what I can do. For you, ok?"

Jacob turned back to his plate as Laila solemnly finished her salad. The crowd in the restaurant seemed to move in tighter on the couple as the patio filled with diners. The idle chatter of laughter and happiness seemed to overwhelm them as they sat in silence. Laila looked around at the couples that seemed to be everywhere, dining at their tables. Everywhere she looked it appeared to be a family in her midst. She couldn't escape the visual of family and happiness everywhere she turned. It was on magazines and in songs and now it was boxing her out in her own restaurant. Love was all around her, yet so intangible.

"Jacob I don't know if I can do this," she said eyes trembling. "If I, or this relationship, has meant anything to you will follow me out to my car shortly after and we can go home. If not, then I don't know."
She stared at him as he dropped his fork in silence. Laila reached into her red leather tote and pulled out some cash and placed it on the table as she turned away. With each step that she took toward her car she fought the urge not to turn and look back. She was too afraid to see if he would be man enough to follow her as she hoisted herself up onto the

leather seat of her truck she waited in vain. She started up her engine not waiting too long, because if he really loved her he would not have even let her leave the table. Two years of her life. Two years of the pain that she had endured, along with her life savings, and to have it all come down to this? A wife?

Her eyes blurred with the stings of rage as she blasted Whitney Houston's why does it hurt so bad on the radio. Why couldn't she just find love? It seemed as though everyone was constantly getting ahead and getting over and not her. She pressed the speed dial of her phone and called for her girl Peanut.

"What's up girl," the baby like voice of her friend Peanut called to her.

"Hey girl, I need a favor," Laila said.

"Anything girl."

"You working over at Fearless now right?"

"Yeah, what do you need?"

"I need to get Lady J promotions in on that party somehow,"

"That may be tough. City is trying to do it really big, its celebrities and industry all the way. Plus City has his own personal ladies he's inviting."

"Look, Peanut you are a part of his PR Team if you can get me a meeting I got the rest."

Laila hung up the phone and exhaled. She was going to need to make some changes fast. Perhaps this was one of them. No man was going to stop her from rising to her rightful place in the society. "If he could let me just walk away like that, everything he said was a bunch of lies."

It was time to get her life back into the swing of things. She was compelled to become a part of this production some way and somehow that was for sure. If anyone could help her do it she knew that Peanut could. She hadn't even had a chance to talk to Phoenix. She wasn't surprised though. Phoenix was known to pull disappearing acts lately. It seemed as though she didn't really need Laila now that she had Dexter and her new campaign. *I guess she is living the high life all over again, she thought. Just that fast. The girl has barely stepped foot in New York and she feels that she can already run the city.* Laila lit up a cigarette a pushed at the bags under her eyes. "I need a spa day this is truly ridiculous." She dialed up Regal salon and made an appointment to see Pronto , Pronto!

"Phoenix isn't the only one that is capable of looking good. Hmmm..I wonder how she is doing any way." She dialed up Phoenix.

"Hey Phoenix. I hadn't heard from you honey. I wanted to grab some lunch. You free?"

"Yes, that shouldn't be a problem. I actually just got back into town this afternoon and I am supposed to have a quick meeting. I wanted to get back as soon as possible so I wouldn't miss it. But after is cool."

"Oh really, who is it with?"

"It's with Big City and Ray Escobando for a spread in Flashy magazine."

"Oh." Phoenix noticed the drop in her friends tone.

"What La? I don't have the job yet. So let's not get excited."

"No I am actually very excited. I was just on the phone with my friend Peanut who is one of City's top executives at his company, if anything is going on, she definitely will know about it. I think I did hear that they were picking some girls for something but I am not sure. But aren't you doing the campaign for DQS Cosmetics? Do you think that Dexter is going to take too kindly to you working for his top rival? He hates City."

Phoenix felt her heart sinking and her head getting tight. How come every time she had good news it seemed as though Laila had something to say about her integrity as if she would do anything to jeopardize what she had worked so hard to get.

"I know, Dexter actually doesn't know."

"Are you serious Phoenix? What if you lose your contract?"

"Laila let's not get to ahead of ourselves. I mean, I was working on things before I met Dexter in order to get my career going on my own. I need to do something on my own by myself. I don't want to shut down my dreams just because the first man I meet in NY wants to throw things at my feet and take me out of my deplorable lifestyle, which isn't all that bad to begin with. I might as well have stayed with Walter."

"First of all Phe, he is not just the first man that you encountered in NY, he is Dexter Stiles, one of the top business men not only in NY but in the country. I mean if you were so concerned about making it on your own, then why did you sleep with him?"

Phoenix narrowed her eyes at her friend. Laila's tone had almost become venomous and personal and she was unsure as to why she was being attacked. "You know what

Laila that is the difference between me and you, I don't care if he is a business man or a mogul or whatever he is. I try to do things for the right reasons. And for your information, I was already signed to my contract before we ever touched."

"Look Phoenix I am your friend, but just to let you know, there is a woman who was engaged to Dexter who is very powerful in this town that is not too happy about having her man snatched from under her."

"Look I didn't snatch any man from anyone. Dexter and I are friends and business partners. I don't get involved with his personal life."

Laila wasn't buying it. Phoenix played the innocent role, but she was more self-serving than anyone that she had ever met. She walked around as if she was the innocuous deer with her eyes caught in the headlights, but she could be cold

260

and calculating and Laila knew that first hand. She didn't care what Phoenix thought or felt she, Laila felt that Phoenix owed her and owed her big time.

"Well, anyway Phe, when are you going to see Big City?"

"Now actually, that is why I need to get off of the phone with you. They are expecting me and I want to get ready."

"I want to meet City and I need your help," Laila said.

"Well, I will see what I can do La. I haven't even met them yet."

Laila raised her voice through gritted teeth, to make sure that she was heard this time.

"Phoenix, I would appreciate this. I need to see City."

Phoenix felt her patience growing thin.

"Fine, La, I have to go now. Some of us have work to do."

261

Phoenix hung up the phone. Laila was getting really pushy.

Phoenix was growing tired of the competition. She just

wanted to do her own thing and come up and never have to

worry about these things ever again.

Chapter Ten

Willie marveled at the monstrosity of the menacing estate in New Jersey that Big City called home. "This is ridiculous," he said. Big City hopped out of his Range Rover smiling. "No, it's just home player." Just home expanded at least 2 acres of land. Its foreboding gray granite and stone structure with a Viking crest insignia firmly planted on the seven foot oak wood doors channeled eighteenth century nobility. It was clear that Big City saw himself as a king and believed that he should literally live like one. As proud of his living quarters as he seemed to be, he was not eager to show Willie his entire home.

"Do you live here all by yourself?"

263

"For the most part. I've been known to host a houseguest or two."

City led Willie into the living room. Willie sank deep into the crevices of the Indian inspired gold and white hand woven silk couch as he listened to City go on.

"Like everything that I do, I like to put a lot of thought into it. I like to put my heart and soul into it and keep it as close to me as possible. I come from a place where it wasn't so pretty even though it may have looked that way on the outside. My mom and pops wasn't too stable. There was abuse and mistrust and all types of things that I promised to avoid when I came up. I wanted a better life."

"Any kids?"

"Nope, no kids. I've just been focusing on my business and my empire. My music is woman enough for me," he joked.

"What motivates you?" Willie said. City walked over to the window and looked out.

"Hate."

"Wow. I never heard that one before. I mean, you have so much. Who do you have to hate? You're successful and rich and you have everything to look forward to, who could you possibly hate."

Big City's eyes were black as he focused in on Willie. "I got hate for all the people that held me down, back, or disrespected me. There's been a lot of them too." He walked over to Willie and snatched the tape recorder from his hands. "I better not see that in print. Or you'll see how much hate I really have. You want to print something, print this. 'Big City is determined to not lose." He looked down at his Rolex. "It's almost ten, let's go downstairs to my studio and meet my new artist before this model comes over that you want me to meet. Her name is Allegria."

Willie's eyes lit up at the sound of her name. He was quite familiar. She was a beautiful young, almond eyed Philipina from Miami. "Oh, man, I was hoping that we would get to see her. We may pose the two of you together for another spread. That would be hot. I know she is going to be amazing. Did you really find her in a strip club?"

"No. I actually met her in Atlanta when I went to church with my mom, last year. She was singing in the choir. Same difference." Willie looked at the hard faced mogul and tried to imagine him in church. That was the thing with the hip-hop community you never knew what was real and what was image. For Big City that image was to maintain a connection

266

with the people that he felt represented his music and aspired to his lifestyle.

City was no fool. He knew the importance of media manipulation. He knew that this cover for Flashy magazine would set the tone for his empire and his estate and he wanted everything to be perfect.

The pair entered Big City's modest studio located in lower region of his tri-level estate. A small, rotund black male sat at the keyboards singing a hook back to Allegria. Her voice tinkled like clinging champagne flutes as she sang the hook with Mitch Wilson. Unlike many other successful producers in the hip-hop industry Mitch didn't have any fancy nickname. He was known not only to be a gifted pianist, but to have a strong ear for harmony and melody. He had worked with some of the most talented and established

267

acts in the industry and always remained humble. Hip-Hop and rappers wasn't really his forte. He was a classically trained musician from the Berklee College of Music but he loved Big City and what he was trying to do and decided to join his team for the Allegria project. He stood and greeted City affectionately when he entered with Willie.

"Man, check out this track City, this is ridiculous!" Mitched jumped up and down. Allegria grinned happily to herself as her girl power anthem pumped through the speakers. "Raising Up" had a military feel to it that made you want to stand up and do something. "I like the drums," Allegria grooved.

Big City listened with his characteristic intense focus and remained expressionless until the song was completed.

"What do you think?" Mitch asked.

"It's not fire. But it's smoldering. I think that you should finish it. Wilson, man, you are a genius!" Allegria faded into the back and began to walk back into the booth and sing the hook that she and Wilson had been working on. She didn't feel the need to wait around for Big City's approval. She knew the way to Big City's heart was through a hit record and she planned to sing her heart all the way to number one.

Willie noticed that the young singer had begun to get quiet and walk back to the booth. He walked over to her, slightly nudging Big City who was wrapped up into what Mitch had to show him next. Allegria knew that process could take a moment. Big City wanted the sound of each track to be pristine and ready to hit the streets if necessary. He didn't like to rely on studio mixing to get his levels right.

He wanted them to be as perfect as possible. That was just who he was. He was a perfectionist.

"You alright?" Willie said placing his hands on her shoulder. Allegria flashed her startled brown eyes. "Of course. Why?"

"No reason. I just wanted to tell you that the song was hot. I like the words. It's like you letting the fellas know that they better be listening up and watching out because you're coming for that number one spot." They laughed together. Yeah it was true. Allegria was trying to come for that number one spot with all that she had. She hoped that Big City noticed but no matter how hard she sang and danced all he seemed to care about was more singing and she wasn't used to that. She couldn't figure him out. He was so nice to her. How come he didn't want more? Was he not into women? Singing was great, but she was looking for real security in her life when this singing stuff dried up.

"I wish the boss could see all I am doing. It's like I am not really good enough for him I don't think," she looked down.

"What are you talking about? He speaks very highly of you. Guess what? I am loving your song a lot. I surprised though," Willie said.

"Why are you surprised?"

"You seem too…I don't know, earthy for Fearless Entertainment. I can see you on Arista or Columbia. Not necessarily a hip-hop oriented label." The young singer fiddled with the rhinestone encrusted FEARless displayed across the thin fabric of her tank top. The subject was obviously a touchy one.

"Yeah, I just want to put my songs out there and get them heard you know? Everyone isn't fortunate enough to have their family as their whole team helping to push them along. Ever since I left home at sixteen I've been trying to make this dream happen and then I finally hooked up with City and my dreams were able to come true. I'm just an artist that is trying to be heard. Trying to get a better life you know?" Willie playfully rubbed the shoulders new young starlet and tried to nudge away that seriousness that surrounded her. He had seen so many artists attempt to come up in the game with her sensibility and sensitivity and never get a shot.

"Well, maybe you will get your wish. You made it this far. I know that City wouldn't have you on his label if you weren't talented." Willie ran the plausibility of running different stories on the young artist. "You never feel slighted that City notoriously takes the credit for the hard work of his artists? I mean, if you want to get your name out there you just may have to fight for it." Allegria stared at him blankly. "I just want to finish my album man," she said putting her headphones on.

"Hey Mitch can you play that slow track for me?"

Willie watched as the naïve singer stepped behind the microphone and began belting out a ballad that Big City had no intentions of releasing.

Willie walked over to Big City.

"She's hot huh?" Big City pointed at

"Yeah, she got talent. Her voice is good," Willie said.

"Yeah, that too," City smiled.

Willie standing mesmerized as she sang. City punched him in the arm. "Don't get any thoughts over there chief."

"No, no? What are you talking about?"

"I see you looking dreamy eyed at her."

"No, I just think that she is talented that's all. I want to profile her."

"You should. Right next to me."

At first glance, one would mistakenly think that Big City didn't want his newly crowned songbird to have a life. This was quite to the contrary. He wanted her to have a life, but he wanted it to be carefully managed. He could see it in her eyes that she suppressed her natural desire to be the next free spirited songstress or whatever she saw herself as. Big City knew what the market needed now.

"No man, I know that we have to run everything through you. I was just noticing that she had heart. That's it."

"Good, just making sure you follow the protocol," Big City said.

Chapter Eleven

Big City's diminutive doorman led Phoenix into the studio where the team was mixing up Allegria's track. Phoenix immediately recognized the stone-faced powerhouse directing his new petite chanteuse from behind the boards. He rose from his chair to shake her hand as she made her way between him and Willie.

"Hey girl, how you doing?" Willie said. "This is Big City, the world famous artist as you already know.

"Phoenix took her seat as Willie went on. "Yeah, this shoot is going to be large. So this could mean big things for you."

City stared at Phoenix as Willie spoke. Her caramel skin looked washed in almond milk. Her wide innocent eyes were hopeful and he found it endearing on a grown woman.

"How old are you?" Big City blurted out.

Phoenix looked startled. "Twenty-eight. Why?"

"You want to be in the music business?"

"I could be," she said coyly. "Right now I am focused on modeling and acting. Currently, I am the new face of DQS Cosmetics."

Big City laughed hysterically. "So Dexter got rid of his babe and moved you in? This could be interesting. Or it could be career suicide. Not that you're not beautiful. You are. It's just that make-up is not where he should be going right now."

277

"What do you mean? DQS style is one of the leading clothing brands for the urban market and Dexter predicts that make-up line will carry on the tradition."

Big City swirled in his chair, focusing his dark eyes on her. "I guess you never got the memo. DQS Entertainment and DQS Style are over. I don't think he will last two more years if he doesn't diversify. He's soft and he alienated everyone that was good around him. But I guess that won't really affect you in the short run. But I don't really think short term, so I wouldn't know anything about that."

"Well, I strongly disagree. Dexter is a genius-"

"Dexter is a bitch."

Willie threw his arms between the two attempting to squelch the rising tension. "Look, let's focus on the matter at hand.

Which is the photo shoot. City, this is the girl I had in mind. If you're interested, I think she is fresh and will be good."

Big City ran the thought of using Dexter's new woman in the photo shoots for the release of his sophomore album and some of his business ventures. Not only would it be great publicity it would boost record sells and crush egos to insinuate that he had somehow had a relationship with the love interest of his biggest rival.

"You familiar with my music?" Big City asked.

"Yes, I am actually. I like Blazin Brains," she said simulating a dance.

He smiled, "You know that's actually one of my favorite songs that radio slept on. So that's really cool that you like it. Really cool."

"Yeah, I loved it. I was hoping that it would be released."

"See," Willie chimed in. "You two have some common ground. I knew you would hit it off. See according to my vision we can spotlight you City and Allegria. Two hot babes. Three powerhouses."

Big City moved in and put his arm around Phoenix. "I like that," he said. "I like Bonnie and Clyde even better. We look very good together."

"No, I am telling you Wade I think that she is the one," Dexter said smiling over at his brother who had paid him a surprise visit to Dexter's Manhattan office.

Wade stared skeptically at his brother. Dexter had talked of getting married many times before and he was curious as to what made this one so different.

"She is smart, beautiful, and feisty. She's all the things that you could want in a woman," Dexter said turning the photo of Phoenix that adorned his desk to his brother. "She kind of reminds me of mom. Don't you think?"

Wade stared at the picture. He saw no resemblance to their mother but decided to pander to his older brother as he had always done. "Sure, maybe she has mom's essence."

Dexter smiled like a proud papa. "Yeah, she has more than mom's essence. She just reminds me of her. And I want to help her to succeed."

"Well Dexter, You know that I support you in all that you do, but what about, Lisa? I mean just two months ago she was your fiancée. And now, what happened to her? You just called off the engagement?" Wade asked.

Dexter rubbed his temples. "That was something that was never going to happen. At least in my eyes."

"But does she know that? Lisa was a good girl. She was gorgeous, talented, and smart. I mean she's all of the things that you said this new girl is. So why are you after her now? I actually liked Lisa. She complimented you well Dexter? You two were a good team together and doing things for your future."

"Man, it takes more than that to have a successful relationship. You know that and I know that. She is a great girl, but there were just parts of her that I was definitely not feeling."

"Like what?"

"I don't know. I-I – didn't trust her for one."

"Why man, what did she ever do to you to make you not trust her?"

"I don't know. We had our situations and disputes and our arguments. I never really felt like she was with me just for me. I always felt like everything was based on what I have and who I was."

"So this new girl, Phoenix, the one that you are taking a major business risk on, is the girl that you trust wholeheartedly?" Wade said. "You don't even know her. You just meet her out of the blue and decided that you are going to play hero and make her your princess?"

Dexter had always admired his brother's knack for getting to the heart of the matter. But this time around Dexter could not be swayed. Wade saw something different in his playboy brother that he had not seen before. He saw a sense of calm and assurance when he spoke of Phoenix. He wondered if his preternaturally loner brother had finally found the love that he had so desperately been in search of.

"No its different man, being with her brings out things that I never knew were there. Even though we can clash heads I still feel like I want to protect her. She's a bit rough around the edges but she has something. I don't know what it is, but I think that she is going to be a star."

"A star at what? Looking good? Anyway Dexter, before you make any rash decisions, I am going to be honest with you. I saw Lisa the other day and she asked about you."

Dexter sighed.

"She looked good. Not necessarily happy, but, good nonetheless."

"Was she wearing her ring?"

"Yeah, she was," Wade said. "I think you should talk to her. You owe it to her, and to yourself to at least talk to her. She's been good to you man for all these years. She's stuck by your side through all of the things that you put her through."

"Wade, you met Debra when you were dating Diane right? "

"Right."

"Ok, but you stopped dating Diane when you met Debra right?"

"Right. But Dex, you and I have always been different."

"What are you talking about? You think that you have the lease on love or something?"

"No, I'm just saying-"

"What? I can't settle down or love somebody good?"

"Man, all I am saying is that you and Lisa seemed to be cut from the same cloth Dex. Of course I want you to be happy. You're my brother. But, you do things that are so extreme sometimes. I think that you meeting this girl and resting the success of your company on her inexperienced shoulders is a risky move."

Part of Dexter felt that his brother was right, but the other half believed that what he was doing was right. He hadn't made it this far without trusting his own judgment.

"Wade, I love you. You're my brother and I respect your opinion. But this time around, I am telling you that you have to trust me. Phoenix is going to be fabulous. Marketing and management love her. We have everything set up and set out to prepare her for a successful start. And, more importantly, if all goes well, I plan to make her my wife. But in the meantime, I guess I have to take care of the small situation with Lisa that I failed to handle. After that, I am a free man." Wade stood and hugged his brother. Seeing his brother leveled –headed and focused again warmed his heart.

"I love you Dex and I wish you the best. If this girl makes you happy then that is who you need to be with." Wade grabbed his jacket and headed for the door. "Well I am going to make my way back down to the shop and get some work done. Debra is expecting me around seven so I want to make sure that I am there. I think she may be pregnant."

"Oh really?" Dexter smiled.

"Yeah, I'm not positive, but it's my gut feeling."

"Congrats man."

"Thanks Dexter. Good luck."

Dexter watched as Wade walked hunched shouldered out of his offices. He often missed having his brother around working side by side with him. It was hard to see him go throw his engineering degree, along with his lucrative position at DQS, out of the window to work as a manager at a garage. True the money was good and there were talks of him possibly owning the place, but Dexter wanted more for his brother. They were supposed to rule DQS Entertainment side by side and live fabulous lives, but his brother had other

plans. Oh well Dexter thought, to each his own.

"Rita, get Lisa Whitaker on the phone will you? I need to talk

to her."

He sat back in his chair with his arms folded behind his head.

Dealing with Lisa was definitely going to be a handful.

Lisa held a cold compress to her head as she lie

sprawled on her couch. She had been sick all morning with an

unknown illness that left her vomiting and feeling dizzy all

day long. She didn't know what was wrong with her but she

knew it wasn't right. She sat up and grabbed the photos lying

on the table of her and Dexter taken in St. Martin last year.

They were both dressed in white and smiling. Or at least she was. Dexter never liked to smile too much in pictures. It just wasn't his thing. Her eyes glistened at the thought. Those were some of the best days of her life. Even if she didn't have Dexter fully, she had what she had and she loved him for that. It was hard to believe that it was over. She flung the photo from her manicured hand into the box and walked over to the large mirror that hung over the fireplace in her foyer.

As usual her make-up was flawless over her equally flawless complexion. Her hair, which she had slightly grown out since she'd last, saw Dexter fell in large, loose ringlets around her shoulders. She practiced different smiles in preparation for any foolishness that Dexter would lay on her today. If it was good she would give him a big smile. If it was bad, he would get a flat 'I don't care' smile.' She rubbed her narrow hips hidden under the blue form fitting dress she wore for the occasion. She had specifically put on some of the jewelry Dexter brought her back from his trip to Morocco with his mother. "This should bring up all good memories," she said tilting her head to the side.

The call from Dexter was unexpected but not surprising. She knew him better than he knew himself. If there was one thing that she was certain of it was that he couldn't be without her. Sure, during the relationship Dexter was known to go away without contacting her for a few weeks or days and return baring gifts. But, they were two of a kind. They were in this thing together. Admittedly she was a little scared this time. His voice over the phone was so serious she felt her stomach twist in knots from his tone.

They had built too much together and she wasn't about to let it all slip away from her now. She held out her hand and admired the diamond that rested on her finger. It was almost like yesterday when Dexter proposed. She had given him an ultimatum. Marry me or I am going to start having sex with other men. She knew his male ego was too competitive for that, and he had a ring resting on her pillow within a week. She would have liked a more romantic proposal. But what was a wedding and a proposal anyway? It was nothing but a three ringed circus. Lisa Whitaker wanted her man and she got him.

She must have been staring off into space for a while because the loud sound of her doorbell startled her. The hallway seemed to extend as she made her way to the front door. She licked her lips and pulled out the best smile that she had, and presented it to Dexter when she opened the door.

"Hey Love," Lisa said extending her hand and guiding him into the airy foyer. "You look nice." Dexter looked around at the house as he made his way comfortably into the living room and sat down resting his feet on the footstool.

Lisa sat down next to him on the couch and drew her legs underneath her. She inhaled the scent of his cologne. The thought of the many nights she waited for that scent to come breezing into the bedroom late at night and hypnotize her. His skin glowed against the white linen of his suit. Dexter fiddled with his watch and looked straight ahead, frightened to meet the pleading gaze of Lisa's eyes. He could feel them bearing into the side of his face.

"Can you get me something to drink?"

Lisa hopped up from the couch. "Scotch and soda?"

"No, just water," he said softly. She walked over to the bar and poured him a glass. As he reached for the glass his eyes fixed on the diamond engagement ring that she still wore on her finger. Lisa quickly withdrew her fingers from the glass and repositioned herself on the couch.

She cleared her throat and lifted her head to meet his gaze. "So Dexter, why exactly did you want to see me?" she asked. "Not that I am not ecstatic to see you, because I am." He sipped his water and looked around the living room. He spotted the photo of the two of them in Cancun and others of her family and friends. They were all such distant reminders of a past that he once shared with a woman that he loved. Looking at those pictures now felt like another life or even being another person. He looked at Lisa.

"You've done a nice job with this place. I'm surprised."

"Why? You didn't think that I could decorate a home?"

"No, I did. I'm just surprised that you took so much care in doing it. You never struck me as domestic."

"I put a lot comforting accents around your Park Avenue place but you were never there to notice."

He placed the water glass on the table and looked at her. She wanted him and he knew it. He found her beautiful and she knew it. That was something that would never change.

"I like your necklace," he said.

"You got this for me-"

"In Morocco," he finished.

"Yeah…"

Dexter couldn't seem to get his voice above a whisper. It felt as if something was lodged in his throat. A part of him wanted to say forget but he couldn't back out now.

"I was hoping that you'd remember the necklace. It was always one of my favorite pieces," she said reaching out and touching his hand. He removed it from under hers.

"So why did you leave our apartment that day? You left the apartment after Mr. Chow's. I couldn't reach you. You left me and I thought that was a disrespectful move on your part," Dexter said frowning.

"First of all I didn't leave you. I was forced out by you and your driving need to crown that woman you just met the princess of DQS Cosmetics."

She turned away from Dexter and looked down at her chest in silence before bringing her eyes back up to him. "Besides, there was a look in your eyes that scared me."

"What look? What are you talking about? The excitement I get when I am about to break a new artist or embark on a new business venture?"

"No, you just looked different when she was sitting next to you."

"How? Tell me!"

"I don't know, just different. I couldn't take it. Look at you sitting here now. You're different and it's only been a couple of months. You look like you love her. Do you?"

"What are you talking about?" Dexter said brushing her off. "Let's stick to the facts. You left me, and you're still wearing my ring."

The tears welled up in Lisa's eyes. "How dare you question me or my ring? With all of the stuff that I put up dealing with you? You grabbed another room, not to mention with the same woman that you went upstairs with at The Lounge, and rubbed in my face at Mr. Chow's. You and I have been through too much together and I planned on staying together."

"Lisa, I left you a message saying that it was over. What are you talking about?"

"How many times have you said it was over and it wasn't Dexter? If I had a dollar for every time you broke up with me I would be as rich as you."

"That's nonsense Lisa. I told you it was over and to move out."

"Yeah and I did. I live here for now. What's your point?"

"The point is it's over. I want the ring back. I mean, you can keep it, but I don't want someone who isn't my fiancé with a rock on her finger that isn't going to marry me."

"What are you saying? *Isn't going to marry you?*" she stared blankly.

"Look Lisa, you are one of the most beautiful women that I have ever been with in my life. I mean you were my girl. You were really my *girl*," he said placing his hand on her shoulder.

"Dexter you don't want this. I mean you told me to go away from you on voicemail. You don't do your fiancé like that. I mean we've known each other for too long-" she stammered.

"I know, I know. I'm sorry Lisa."

"Dexter I love you. I have always loved you. We were supposed to spend our lives together. Everyone thinks that we're great together and share a special connection. You did too."

"Yeah I did, but people change," he said. "You know as well as I do that we fought too much and we just couldn't seem to get on the same page."

"Dexter everyone has their disagreements. What do you expect?"

Dexter's eyes shifted from the pictures to Lisa to the wall and back to Lisa. He tuned her out as she went on and on about their love and relationship. His mother and her sisters.

"Dexter? Dexter? Do you hear me talking to you? Are you just going to ignore me like you always do?"

"What do you want from me? People change. Shit happens and you have to deal with it. I'm sorry Lisa. I moved on."

"You're sorry Lisa? That's all you have to say. What about my mother? Your mother? Our families and friends? The people that believed that this shit was forever? What about the bullshit period? I gave you the best sex of my life. That means nothing to you? You're just going toss me to the side like I am some kind of late model truck just because you met some random female?"

"Lisa look," he said calmly. "It has nothing to do with her. This has to do with us. I apologize for not ending it face to face initially. That's why I am here now. I am here to right the wrongs of my past. I don't want to marry you because I think that you belong with someone else."

"Don't speak for me Dexter. I belong with you. I know it," she said pulling his face toward hers kissing him deeply. For a moment he felt himself go weak.

He grabbed her face in his hands and looked in her eyes, "Ok, then I will speak for myself. Lisa, you are not the one for me."

"Why? Tell me why? Why would you tell me wanted to marry me, if I wasn't the one?"

"I don't know why Lisa," he said shaking his head. "I don't know. I'm sorry. Your perfect but I just can't be with you anymore. I can't." She reached over and wrapped her arms around his neck and began to cry. Dexter rubbed her back as her body shook. "You don't love me anymore Dexter? Tell me you don't love me anymore and I will go away," she said gently nibbling at his neck.

It was hard to deny how good she felt against his chest. She was so small that he could wrap his arms around her twice. But, he thought of the night he sat up watching Phoenix sleeping next to him as gentle as a lamb and at that moment Lisa's nibbles felt insignificant. He thought of the life that he and Lisa had built and realized that he was the one who helped her build it too.

He pushed her from his neck and stared her in the eyes. "Listen, I will always respect what we had together and what we built. But, I just don't feel that passion. I'm going to let you go."

"Then why are you here Dexter. Why did you come here?"

"Because I wasn't sure what I felt. Everything seemed to point to you. To stay with you. It just seemed right. But my heart is telling me something else."

Lisa stood from the couch and slapped him. "What do you know about heart? You don't have a heart. All you do is break hearts."

Dexter rubbed his jaw fighting back the urge to release his rage but he had too much to lose.

"I don't know about my heart. But, this is the first time I've wanted to find out." Dexter braced himself. Lisa drew her arm back and smacked his face.

"Get out!"

"I'm sorry-"

"Fuck you. Get out, get out! Get the fuck out of my house. And take your fucking bullshit ass ring with you!" she screamed tossing the diamond in his lap.

Dexter rose from the chair dodging the piercing screams that threatened to shake his confidence as he walked to the door. Asshole, heartbreaker, loser, cruel....

He had heard them all before and let the comfort of her disgust carry him out of the door and into his Mercedes.

Phoenix pried her hand away from Big City's grip as she slid into the town car that waited to take her into the city. "I'll call you," he called out as the car pulled away. She had already stayed two hours longer than she had planned to. Willie was long gone when Big City asked her to stay for a while longer so they could get to know each other better. Phoenix knew that it was probably not a good idea but when he told her that he was in talks to start his own production company she couldn't resist. Big City seemed to have more on his mind than movies, but Phoenix was in no mood to hear about it. She just wanted to get back to the Dexter's townhouse and get ready for the DQS Cosmetics event that was to take place at the Puck Building later that evening. She picked up her phone that was ringing in her purse. She saw Dexter's number flashing and braced herself for what she knew would be a barrage of questions.

"Hi Dexter," she chimed.

"Hi sweetheart," he said. "Where are you? I thought you were going to meet Brooke and the glam squad over at your hotel so you could get ready for tonight. Where have you been? I thought I told you to keep your phone on you at all times." Phoenix clutched the phone as a million excuses raced through her mind. She wanted to lie to him, but she thought better of it and decided she should tell the truth. She had to tell him at the right time. "I'll be at the hotel in thirty minutes. Tell everyone to hold on. You know the queen must be the last to arrive and the first to leave right?"

Dexter laughed. She had only been signed to DQS Cosmetics and she was already pulling diva antics. She learned quickly. "Ok, I will have my assistant let them know you're on the way. No matter what though you need to be there by 10:30 so we can introduce you to the investors, staff, and some of my

307

business associates. I want you looking good baby," he cooed.

Phoenix laughed. "I'll be there. As a matter of fact I am looking forward to it. I will make sure I am extra beautiful just for you."

Phoenix sank down in her seat after she hung up the phone. She felt confused about tonight and about how Big City looked at her. He kept telling her that Dexter Stiles' career was almost over and if she had any sense at all she would try and make her own money. That was all she ever tried to do was make her own money and take care of herself but it seemed that either men or her heart always got in the way.

Phoenix hopped out of the town car and rushed into the Soho Grand. She was immediately rushed by Brooke,

Damone and Viv her fabulous glam squad. "Where have you

been Miss lady? We have been waiting for over an hour for

you?" Damone said plopping her in a chair.

"Sorry. Sorry. I have no excuse," Phoenix said. "I am ready to

get to work. I am 100% at your mercy right now. Whatever

you guys want. The traffic was horrible."

Viv eyed her suspiciously. "C'mon let's get started. Don't

make it a habit." She had seen girls like her come and go and

she hoped Phoenix made the most of this moment. Phoenix

continued to apologize profusely for the next twenty minutes

until Damone finally told her to "Relax." The team went

retro and settled on an all-white sixties inspired jumpsuit with

platinum accessories. Brooke added waist length extensions

and Viv lightly applied tinted moisturizer and created a

dramatic eye. The trio gave themselves a high five for the

work they had created and Phoenix felt ready to unveil herself at the party.

As she glanced at her reflection in the mirror she felt a small pang of fear rush over her. It seemed as if it was only a matter of minutes that her life had been changed. She had come to New York to get her life back on track and hopefully make a few contacts in the industry and then eventually get a few gigs, but there was nothing that prepared her for this. Tonight she would be introduced to some of the most important people in New York Society and she didn't know if she deserved it.

"C'mon princess. We have to get you to the ball," Damone said snapping her out of thoughts. "And from what I understand, or according to all of these messages I keep getting honey, your prince charming is waiting on you."

"But why-" Phoenix tried to protest.

"Honey, Dexter Stiles is a smart man. He is a wealthy man and he has been all over this world. He would never make a decision if it wasn't right. You're absolutely perfect," Damone smiled giving her a knowing look. "Now let's ride out Ms. Diva."

Phoenix rushed out of the hotel feeling as if she were off to her own wedding. Perhaps there was something in the air but she knew that tonight would be a night that she would never forget.

Chapter Twelve

Laila paced back and forth in front of the Puck

Building as she tried to find another way to side step security

and make her way into the event. She wasn't sure why she

wasn't able to get on the list, but she had tried to get a hold

of Phoenix all day but she wouldn't return her calls. She

wished Jacob would have at least stayed with her until she got

into the venue but he was so impatient that he left her

standing there looking like an idiot once security denied her

entry. "That's a sign babe. It's not happening tonight. Let's go

somewhere else and hang out." Laila was incredulous that he

would give up so easily and want to leave one of the most

important events of the summer. Laila struggled with her

phone as she waved him on. She was determined to get through to someone.

"No. You go ahead without me. I need to get in here. There are some contacts that I want to make. Plus I should be here to support my girl right?" Jacob shook his head as he walked to the curb and hailed a cab. "Good luck with that."

Laila fought the urge to call out after him. Lord knows where he would probably end up tonight. Her career depended on it. Laila pulled a cigarette from her purse as she attempted to call Phoenix again. She angrily blew smoke into the breeze when she felt a hard push in her back from behind. "Excuse me miss. Make a path! Make a path!" security said as they briskly ushered in the smiling Phoenix to the front of the line and into the building. Laila stood there with her mouth open, to in awe to shout, as her friend stepped in behind the velvet ropes. "Phoenix! Phoenix!" Laila waved hysterically. A bystander stared at her like she was a thirsty fan. "Unbelievable," Laila said. "To think she wouldn't have even known Dexter had I not taken her to the party and now she is too big to invite me to her party?" Laila tried Jacob's phone but it went straight to voicemail. She knew what that meant. She was on her own tonight. This night was turning out to be one of the worst nights of her life. "I may be down," she said. "But I am definitely not out." With a flick of her long blond hair she hopped in a cab and smiled. If her dear friend didn't know that crossing friends was a very bad thing she soon would. "Hi, I'm going to the W hotel in Times Square. Thank You."

Dexter stopped mid-sentence when Phoenix entered the room. Arnold Clayburn head of DQS marketing could have been speaking Spanish for all he cared. He watched her from across the room similarly to the first day he had ever seen her. She was effervescent and at that moment he knew without a shadow of a doubt that he had made the right decision to not only cast her as his new model but hopefully in the role of his leading lady. He had to admit that he wasn't too happy about being left in the dark about her whereabouts but he didn't want to start pulling in the reigns on her so soon in the relationship. She worked the room effortlessly and he knew that is what she always wanted to do and he let her have her moment.

"Dexter, you ok man?" Dexter looked at Arnold like he was seeing him for the first time. "I'm sorry Arnold, would you please excuse me. I'll be right back."

"But Dexter, we are in the middle of a discussion here-"

Dexter was already making his way through the crowd to Phoenix when he noticed a large man give Phoenix a kiss on the cheek while letting his hand languor on the small of her back. Phoenix politely pushed the man away when he tried to whisper something in her ear, but the man was persistent. Dexter's felt his face grow hot. He tried to keep his cool but found himself feeling slightly jealous watching the scene play out. The man began to laugh as he turned away and Dexter caught a glimpse of his menacing face. It was Big City. How the hell did he get in here? Dexter started to motion to security but thought better of it and decided that he should walk over to City himself.

City was already making his way away from Phoenix when Dexter tapped his shoulder. "What's up Sean? I see you made it to the party?"

Big City rolled his eyes. "Oh was this exclusive? I just walked in. I didn't know," he laughed.

"Yeah it is. It's invite only and I don't recall having put you on any list."

City looked over at Phoenix and raised his glass. "Yeah, your girl told me about it. She was in such a rush to get here. I figured I'd find out what the big deal was about," he said gesturing around the room. "Plus I wanted to check out Phoenix and make sure that she was doing alright, you know?"

Dexter moved in closer to City and looked him square in the eye. "What goes on between me, my model, and my company has nothing to do with you."

"Wow Mr. Stiles, the way you sweating right now I would've thought that she was a little bit more than just your model. I mean she does have a nice-"

"Watch yourself Sean. She's my investment."

"Maybe that's the problem Dexter. You only see women as investments." Phoenix tried to let the two men handle their dispute themselves, but the last words that fell from Dexter's lips upset her. Was that all she was to him? An investment? When he took her to California and they made love she thought that she was more than just his investment. She didn't understand what kind of game that Dexter Stiles was playing with her emotions but she didn't like it.

318

She grabbed a drink off one of the trays that the waiter was carrying and began to sip then quickly gulp. She grabbed two more and gulped them both down in anger. Her head felt light. "Excuse me," she said walking away from her guests and towards Dexter and City. The men stopped their conversation as she stood there with her eyes blazing at Dexter. "I don't mean to break up this man battle you seem to have going on but if you haven't noticed I've been standing here by myself for awhile."

"Wow Dex I see you haven't changed. Still putting the ladies on the back burner when it comes to your needs, huh?" Phoenix put her hand out as if to silence Big City from doing any more damage. "I think I can handle this on my own City thank you."

"Whatever you say baby," he said. "Let me know when you ready to suit up for the majors. See you Friday." Big City waved for his entourage to follow him as he left the party. Dexter sneered at Phoenix. "What's going on Friday? You and City have plans? What's going on here?"

Phoenix shook her head. This was the not the way that she wanted to tell Dexter about the photo shoot. His eyes searched hers for answers as she turned away from him.

"What's going on Phoenix? I set up this whole night for you. I bring you into my circle and I find out at my own party that you are dating the one man in this industry that wants to see my downfall? What's up with that? What kind of game are *you* playing?" Dexter said through gritted teeth.

Phoenix's lips trembled with fear. She couldn't stand the pain in his eyes. She wanted desperately to speak but she didn't think that Dexter would understand. "Dexter, please don't try to turn this on me. Besides, it's not even what you think," she said reaching for his arm. Dexter was stiff to her touch.

"Oh yeah?" His piercing eyes never left her face as she tried to look down at her shoes. "Hey Dexter man, we got to get Phoenix up to the stage. It's time for her introduction," Arnold said.

He looked at Dexter and back to Phoenix. "Everything ok here man?"

Dexter nodded his head.

Arnold hesitated then put his arm out for Phoenix to hold onto.

"Well, then let me escort this lovely lady to the stage. You look beautiful by the way." Phoenix pushed out a meek smile. As she walked to the stage she worried about her future with DQS Cosmetics and more importantly she worried about her future with Dexter. The look in Dexter's eyes made her heart feel like it was breaking. She wanted to tell him the truth but she didn't want him or anyone else to feel like they controlled her.

Watching him talk to Big City and listening to what Big City had to say about Dexter brought thoughts of Walter back to her mind. She didn't want to live that way anymore. She wanted to be free to be her own person.

Phoenix barely heard the applause when they spoke her name and asked her to say a few words. She was gently nudged by her the DQS publicist Jamaica to take her place at the microphone. Phoenix looked out over the applauding crowd and scanned the room for Dexter. "I wanted to say thank you to DQS Entertainment and especially to Mr. Dexter Stiles who has given me the opportunity of a lifetime by allowing me to work with him and represent his company, and young women of color all over the world. DQS Cosmetics is a global brand and it is truly an honor. As many of you may know this has been a long road for me. To finally see something great come out my humble beginnings is amazing. Having a dream come true like this is more than I could have imagined and I hope I do it justice. So Mr. Stiles wherever you are tonight, I thank you for making a girl's dream come true. Thank you everybody." Phoenix was escorted off the stage by Jamaica and the DJ cranked up the music a little louder giving the attendees the permission to party the night away. Phoenix was greeted by well wishers at every side but she could not escape the sinking feeling that she had hurt Dexter beyond repair and she had to find him and make it up to him.

Laila stomped into the W hotel and made her way into the crowded lounge and scanned the room. She was taking a big risk by being here but this was something she had to do. If Phoenix thought that she was going to come to New York and show no respect for the people that helped her get

to where she was then she was about to have a serious wake
up call. She made her way to the bar past the wobbling female
gamine's that migrated toward the hipsters and businessmen
in suits. She knew the scene all too well. She was well aware
of girls putting on their evening best in hopes of landing a big
fish and ride the elevator straight to the penthouse. Normally
she would indulge, but tonight was about business.

"French Martini please," she snapped at the
bartender. It was her signature drink and she knew that she
would need it if she would ever be able to pull off what she
was about to do. Laila nearly choked on her drink when she
spotted the leggy Lisa Whitaker stride towards her direction.
She hadn't seen the former beauty queen and model in a long
time but she seemed to be more radiant than the last time
she'd see her. As promised she wore a silver mini dress

dripped in all the diamonds that she owned. Laila quickly stood up and waved her over.

"Laila James?" Lisa said curiously.

"Yes. Thank you so much for coming. I know you probably don't remember me," Laila stammered.

"Yeah, you're right," said Lisa. "But you sounded pretty desperate on the phone. So I came."

Laila realized that Lisa Whitaker did not meet with people unless it was for a very good reason, and if she didn't get to that reason soon enough she would walk out the door.

"Listen, I know you have better things to do on a weeknight besides sitting here and meeting me at the W. But as I mentioned on the phone, you and I have an enemy in common."

"An enemy?" said Lisa. "Who said I had any enemies? You said you had information on Dexter. Although I can't imagine why or how," Lisa stared at her blankly.

"Well, I happen to know that you and Dexter were engaged and now he is playing Daddy Warbucks to a certain girl that used to be my best friend but is truly nothing more than an opportunist who would do whatever it took to get to her goals."

Lisa flipped her long hair over her shoulders and stared coldly into Laila's eyes. "Look, when you first contacted me I will admit I was skeptical. I mean, we met *once*? In passing right?" Laila nodded. "However, I if what you are saying is true, I think that Dexter should know about this. He was my fiancé and I don't want anyone to hurt him. But how I am supposed to believe that what you are saying is true? Dexter seems to think that she walks on water, and I know Dex very well. Once he gets set on something he won't let go until he's seen it through. Unfortunately, I think he wants to see this through," Lisa said her eyes glistening with tears.

"Well, like you said, Dexter deserves to know who he is dealing with right? Well, I bet he doesn't know that Phoenix has been going behind his back and making deals with Big City?" Laila said.

"What exactly is she doing with Big City if she is supposed to be doing a modeling campaign with Dexter?"

"That's what I am saying Lisa. Phoenix Mitchell is greedy. She wanted to cut her own deal on the side so that she could make an even bigger name for herself. She doesn't know how to be loyal and she doesn't know how to be patient. I am telling you I have a plan that will get you back with Dexter where you belong and Phoenix running so quickly out of this town she'll wish she never set foot in New York."

"So what do you propose that we do?" Lisa said.

Lisa waved the bartender over and ordered two glasses of champagne. "Lisa you just leave that up to me." Laila pulled her vibrating phone from her clutch. "Oh look who has just left a message? Our favorite girl. Oh and she says that she has left the party and wants to see me. At. Her. Hotel."

"Well if Phoenix is at her hotel room alone. Then that means she can't be with Dexter right?" Lisa asked.

"Right," said Laila. "But you can. I have a gut feeling that he may need a little comforting tonight." The two women grabbed their champagne glasses. "Let's make a toast," Laila said. "To you and your return to happiness."

"Cheers. Thank you Laila, I thought this was going to be a boring evening, but it's turned out to be my lucky day."

Phoenix decided to send Dexter one more text message before leaving him a voicemail message. If she knew that she was going to feel this way, she would have never agreed to do a photo shoot with Big City. Right now she realized that not only did she not want to be alone, but she wanted to be with Dexter.

"Dexter, it's me Phoenix. Listen, we need to talk. I know that you are thinking that I am trying to mess you over by talking to Big City but it's not like that," she sighed. "Listen baby, I can't do this without you. This is not about the job. This is about us, L.A., the night we met. Just call me ok." Phoenix curled up in a ball on the bed and tried not to cry. For the first time in her life she felt that she might lose the one person that she truly cared about. Just as she was

331

about to call up room service to have them bring her a bottle of champagne she heard a knock at the door.

"Go away," she yelled reaching for the phone. The knock persisted. She angrily marched over to the door. "What do you want," she screamed as she flung open the door. Dexter stood in front of her with his head slightly lowered and his dark eyes looking up at her. Phoenix stood at the door biting her trembling lips. As Dexter moved closer she fell into his arms and sobbed.

"I'm so sorry Dexter. I'm so sorry." Dexter stood her up straight and held her at arm's length.

"Why did you lie to me?" he said. Phoenix turned her head away and tried not to look into his eyes but he held her chin with his hands. "After all I've done for you, why did you lie to me?"

332

"Dexter, I didn't lie. I told you that it was not what you thought and it isn't. City-"

"Oh, it's not even just about Big City baby girl. When were you going to tell me about Flashy Magazine? I thought you weren't going to do that shoot?" Phoenix backed away from him. She needed to get away from his accusations but it felt as if the walls were closing in on her. Dexter moved toward her.

"Oh you thought that I wouldn't find that out huh? This is my city. I know everything that goes down in it and I know everything that goes down with you Phoenix."

"Dexter, please let me explain."

"Let you explain huh? You are on a contract with my name on it. This is my brand and reputation on the line. The girl that I sign to be the face of anything with my name attached

333

to it would not be such a desperate woman posing for Flashy Magazine with Big City. He's the one man I can't stand. That right there is the ultimate betrayal." Phoenix's back was now against the wall as Dexter's eyes burned a hole through her.

"Dexter, why are you looking at me like I'm the enemy? I'm not your enemy."

"You are my enemy Phoenix. You've shown me that," he said. "I want to fire you right now. But, consider this one on me. Your contract is for a year. I hope it was worth it."

As Dexter turned to walk out Phoenix grabbed his arm. "You can judge me all you want. But I don't think there's anything wrong with a girl trying to put away a little something for herself. Here I was thinking that you were different. I see you are just like all the rest."

"Oh yeah, and how is that Phoenix?"

334

"Controlling."

"If you want to call someone recognizing talent, showing they care and wanting to give a person a chance controlling then you call it what you want."

"Dexter you were fine with me being successful as long as you were the one handing it to me, but as soon as I wanted to step out and be even bigger than even you could imagine you become upset with me."

"Phoenix the last thing I wanted to do was control you. I think it's a shame that out of all the things you would think that I wanted to do with you, you would pick controlling you as one of them. Have a good night," he said.

Phoenix held her breath as he placed his hand on the door. Dexter stood facing the closed door for what seemed like forever before he finally walked out.

Phoenix fell lifelessly to the floor. She wanted to run after Dexter and tell him that she loved him, but she didn't know how. How could she tell him that she was not the woman that he thought he knew, or even worse, maybe she was just like all the rest?

Chapter Thirteen

Laila stepped off onto the elevator of the Soho Grand leading to Phoenix's room and nearly ran into a clearly furious Dexter Stiles storming out. Laila's heart sank fearing that it might be too late and she would find Phoenix happily packing her belongings and moving in with Dexter. She wanted to send Lisa a text and tell her to rethink her plans of surprising Dexter at his penthouse suite but she decided to wait until she could find out what was happening with her own eyes. When she went to knock on the door she found that the door was slightly open and Phoenix was finishing up a call, and hurriedly throwing her clothes into a bag. Laila pushed the door opened as a startled Phoenix looked over her shoulder with a flat, "Hey girl."

Laila stepped over the pile of clothes that was centered in the middle of the floor and all over the bed. "Hey girl," Laila said looking around in amazement. "What in the world are you doing?" Phoenix crossed in front of her to grab more things and stuff them into a bag.

"What does it look like I am doing? I'm packing." Laila grabbed her shoulders. "I can see that, but why? Where are you going?"

Phoenix wrenched away and continued packing. "I'm going to a friend's house. I have to get the hell out of here. I can't stay here anymore so I am leaving." Laila sat down in the chair opposite the bed and watched Phoenix angrily rush around the room.

"Phoenix wait, what happened? I mean, I saw Dexter leaving as I walked out and he didn't look too happy. Is everything alright between you two?"

"I don't want to talk about my boss right now, I just want to pack my stuff up and leave. I have to get ready for my fitting with Flashy magazine tomorrow as well as meet with the team over at DQS Cosmetics and start shooting and doing the photos. So I have a crazy busy week and I want to rest and get ready."

"Well you said that you were staying with a friend, how come you didn't stay with me?"

"Sorry Laila, I didn't want to stay in Brooklyn you know?"

Laila gave Phoenix a side glance as she tried to hide her disgust at her friend's pretentiousness. "Oh, I'm sorry is Brooklyn not good enough for you anymore? I guess not. I see you are this big supermodel right now and have no time for people that helped you or cared about you."

Phoenix stopped packing and rubbed her forehead. "Look Laila, can we not make this about you right now? I happen to be going through some real traumatic stuff. I don't know if I still even have a contract, guaranteed money, and even worse I might have messed up with Dexter." Laila put on her best concerned face.

"So you mean to tell me that you and Dexter are no more?"

"I mean to tell you that, whatever we were, thanks to me, we are no more. I am sure that makes you ecstatic," she said sarcastically.

"That does not make me happy. I mean, I felt like you and Dexter were rushing into things but, I didn't want to see you hurt."

Phoenix tossed the remainder of her things in her bag and zipped it closed. The phone next to her bed purred gently. "I better get that," Phoenix said. Phoenix placed her delicately manicured hand on the receiver and put the phone to her ear. "Yes. I am ready. Just tell them to grab all of the bags in the room and I will be right down. Thank you." Phoenix turned to Laila as she grabbed her Louis Vuitton bag. "Look thanks for coming over. You're a good friend. I have to go, but I will give you a call tomorrow or later this week or something. Is that okay?"

Laila stood up and hugged her friend. "Of course that is okay. I mean you know I am here for you," she said

341

pushing Phoenix's hair out of her face. "You know I always have been."

Phoenix looked away. "I know."

"I would like to know where you are staying though. Can you at least tell me that much since it is not with me?"

"I can't girl. I just need to keep this close, but look, I love you. I will call you as soon as I can. We need to do a girls night again," Phoenix kissed her cheek. The bellboy entered the room and Phoenix pointed to the bags. "I am going to walk down. Take care ok." Phoenix bolted out of the room as Laila stood in the middle of the room looking confused. She dialed Lisa's number and she answered on the first ring. "Hey Lisa," she breathed into the phone.

"What's the word," Lisa said sounding slightly bored.

"Well, this might be easier for you than I thought. I heard it straight from our girl's mouth. She and Dex are no more. So you may want to make your way uptown and make sure that he doesn't have a moment to pine over her. Maybe remind him a little about the big mistake he made."

"Humph," Lisa said. "This does sound interesting although if I know Dexter he is definitely not uptown. He is somewhere close to family if he is truly upset. But, I don't know. Laila, I mean the last time I spoke with Dexter he seemed to be really into this girl and so over me. I don't if I want to play myself like that."

Laila rolled her eyes. "Look are you just going to let this girl steal your man, dump him and leave him cold like that? It only makes you look bad. Lisa, go get your man and teach this girl that she can't just come into New York and do whatever she wants to people."

Lisa sighed. "You're right. I am going to find Dexter. You know Laila I will admit, I didn't really think too much of you before, but now I think you are a pretty cool girl. However, I think I can take it from here."

"Anytime Lisa, like I said before I have always been a fan of yours and I respect you greatly. Maybe we could you know, hang out sometime? We are both in the industry and all. It truly is all about who you know." Laila didn't hear anything on the other end and thought she had lost Lisa. "Lisa?"

"Oh sorry, Laila, I missed what you said. I can't talk and do make-up at the same time so I will talk to you next time.

Thanks again honey." Lisa hung up the phone leaving Laila feeling a little stunned.

"Wow, those stuck up women will never change," she said heading for the bathroom to reapply her lipstick. As she was washing her hands she noticed a letter with Phoenix's name on it and a small Tiffany & Co.'s box beside it.

"Wow, this girl is so ungrateful she can afford to leave jewelry behind?"

Laila called Phoenix but the phone went straight to voicemail. She was going to leave a message but thought better of it and decided to call the front desk.

"Hi, this is Laila James and I am Phoenix Mitchell's new assistant. I noticed that Ms. Mitchell left behind a very valuable item on the vanity. Is there a way that you can tell me where the car took her and her things? You see I am supposed to deliver this stuff to her, but I will lose my job if they know that I misplaced the information." The girl on the other line gave her an address to a residence in New Jersey. "Thank you so much," Laila gushed. "You have no idea how much you've saved my job."

Laila hung up the phone and twirled the box in her hand. "Oh Phoenix, what are you up to now?" Laila placed the unopened letter in her purse and fingered the red ribbon on the box and decided to open it. She stared in amazement at the delicate pink diamond solitaire surrounded by smaller diamonds on the white gold necklace. Laila tried to slip it over her ring finger but it was too small. "Dammit fat fingers," she said placing the ring back into the box. Her curiosity was peaked as she removed the letter from her purse. She had to know who this mystery suitor was that was

346

sending her friend gifts. *Dear my / sweet Phoenix, I knew that there was a God when he finally decided to bring you back to New York. When I saw you a while back at Mr. Chow's with Dexter Stiles, I wanted so desperately to run over to you and take you in my arms. I knew that that was not the right moment. You're all grown up it seems. I wanted to send you a gift to congratulate on your new contract and let you know that I am doing much better now. More importantly I haven't forgotten about you and all that we shared. I hope you enjoy the diamond. I will be in contact soon. Forever Yours, Walter.*

"Oh my goodness!" Laila screamed holding the letter. "Walter Deveroux? This is crazy. I almost feel sorry for the poor bastard," she said placing the letter and box into her bag and heading out the door. The thought that Walter Deveroux could possibly return to Phoenix's life was almost too hard to contain. Laila was going to need a cigarette and a glass of wine to figure out how to handle this. She was a little surprised that Walter hadn't moved on by now considering the fact that Phoenix had left him cold. "No wonder Phoenix is creeped out. He is obviously missing a few screws. But he does have nice taste in jewelry. But still. Scary," she twirled the necklace in her finger. "I should warn her. Or not. The plot only thickens."

Dexter brushed his mother's hair and placed a warm cup of chamomile tea in her hand. Corrine brought the liquid to her mouth and winked at Dexter. "I see you took a note from my play book," she said.

"When you and your brother were little I used to give you chamomile tea to calm you down so I could get some peace at night. I would've given you liquor but we needed it," she said laughing.

"Well me and Wade knew something was up even back then. You fooled no one ma."

"I hope you're not giving me this tea to knock me out or anything Dexter."

"Of course not mom, I just thought it would relax you. Also, I just wanted to take care of you a little bit you know? That's why I moved you back into your house and got the nurse to come by so you can be by your stuff. I wish I could have you stay with me, but I'm so in an out I can't really be there-"

Corrine placed her cup on the night stand and looked at son who had been speaking but looking far off. Ever since

Dexter was a child she knew that he had a tendency to hide his innermost feelings and keep them to himself. For years after Dexter's father had been long gone, he felt that it was his responsibility to save the world and be the father of the family even though Wade was the oldest. Dexter rubbed his temples and exhaled deeply.

"Son, what's on your mind? You look like your over there suffering and I'm the one with cancer. What is it? Talk to me."

"Nothing ma. It just seems like when I try to do the right thing and make my life right and put all the scandal behind me it doesn't work for me. The bad thing is that once you get a glimpse of the promise land, or the good life, you can't go back. You can want the good life, but if the good life wants no part of you, what can you do?"

"Dexter this sounds like you're talking about more than a good life because if you look around you have a great life. I know your brother told me that you are no longer with Lisa. Now you have another young lady that you want to bring home. Does that have anything to do with it?"

"Well, I know you're probably disappointed about Lisa-"

"No, I'm not upset. I was not a big fan of hers anyway. I thought she was a little cold. She seemed too perfect like she wasn't human or something." They both laughed.

"Yeah, she was definitely proper. No doubt about that," Dexter said. "But she did love me. Even if it was in her own way. I felt like she got me. She got what I was about and what I was trying to do."

"Dexter you liked that girl because everyone else did. She didn't make you laugh like Rih Rih did."

351

"Ma, Rih Rih was my girlfriend in the 8ᵗʰ grade. I mean nothing is going to be like that."

"Well you haven't had a real love since," she said.

"Well she broke my heart too. So I was cool on girls for awhile," he laughed.

"So now you found another girl and you're afraid she is going to break your little heart all over again aren't you?" Dexter looked solemnly passed his mother.

"I wanted to give Phoenix the world. She seemed to want it, but not be able to get it. And I wanted to give it to her. But that wasn't good enough for her. Instead she wanted to go behind my back and toss what I wanted to do to the side. I couldn't make her happy so I let her go. I mean we're going to still work together but emotionally I am going to let her do her job and then I am going to fall back."

352

Corrine grabbed her son's hand. "Dexter you are just like your father. You know that? Let me tell you. Before I met your daddy all I wanted to be was a singer. I used to sing everywhere that I went. All the time. I met your daddy and he was trying to be some kind of records man but turned out he was only a simple family man at heart. He didn't really want too much to do with the world. I think it made him nervous or something," Corrine said shaking her head. "Anyway he promised me the world and I believed him. More importantly he promised to take me around the world so I could sing, but I swear he knocked me up so quick it was all over for me. After that, he wanted me all to himself. I never had a chance. But I sure did love him. He took care of us."

"Mom, I'm not dad. Like I said I wanted Phoenix to have the world. I wasn't trying to hold her back."

"Yeah, but you wanted to be the one that controlled her world. You have to let her spread her wings and discover what she wants to do. If it's meant to be she'll come back to you. But more importantly son, if this girl means so much to you, you need to let her know. Make sure that she doesn't get away."

Dexter smiled at his mom. She always knew the right thing to say but this time he was going to handle this himself. Phoenix had made him look like a fool. He couldn't allow that. Corrine had begun to doze off and Dexter kissed her forehead and walked out of the room. He heard the doorbell ring downstairs. *Who could be coming over here at this hour?* He thought. "Arnelle can you grab that door? Tell whoever it is my mother is sleeping."

Dexter removed his shirt and went into the office. His lean biceps flexed as he sat at his computer, in his white tank top, and began to work. Getting work done at his mother's house was sometimes easier than working in Manhattan. He figured he would lay low in Brooklyn for a few days until the DQS Cosmetics photo shoot started up. He probably wouldn't over see it on a day to day as he had initially planned. But he did intend on making sure that his vision was carried out throughout the campaign. No matter what he felt for Phoenix, he knew that he was capable of maintaining a professional relationship with her.

Dexter sat down at his desk and began to scroll through emails.

"I guess I still know you better than you thought," a sultry voice said from the doorway. Dexter looked up in

355

surprise at a coyly smiling Lisa. He hadn't expected to see her but he couldn't deny that she looked incredibly sexy standing in the doorway. She was grinning seductively with a short red mini dress that hugged every curve on her body. Dexter suddenly realizing that he was nearly naked reached for his shirt.

"Please, don't cover up for me," Lisa said shutting the door behind her. "I don't know when I'll ever get to see you like this again," she laughed. "Especially now that you belong to someone else."

"Who told you I was with someone else? Dexter asked.

"I believe you did Dexter. Well, the last time I saw you anyway."

"Well, things change. You know that," Dexter said looking her body up and down.

"Is that so?" she said.

"Yeah."

Lisa walked slowly over to Dexter and sat on the edge of his desk and looked him in his eyes. Dexter could hear himself breathing as Lisa crossed her long legs in front of him. Although she had a look of concern on her face she playfully ran her hands along the inside of her thighs as she focused her eyes on his. This was a tease that always seemed to get Dexter every time. She knew that he had always loved her legs. They were long and toned due to her hour long Pilates sessions. He loved it when she wrapped them around his body when they made love. Before he met Phoenix he never thought there was a woman that could match him sexually the way that Lisa did. When he and Lisa made love she was insatiable and she gave all of herself to him freely.

357

The one thing that he could say about Lisa is that, unlike Phoenix, she held nothing back from him. Dexter realized that he and Lisa had been staring at each other for what seemed like forever before he finally spoke.

Dexter's voice was husky. "Lisa what are you doing here?"

Lisa gathered her hair in her hands and gently placed it on one side of her shoulder. "I'm here for you Dexter. Remember I told you that I would never let anyone hurt you?"

"Who said I was hurt?"

"Not only did I hear it through the grapevine, I can look at you and see that you are going through something right now. I know you. Remember?"

Dexter began to protest but Lisa stopped him by putting her long manicured fingernail against his lip. "No

Dexter, don't say anything. I just want you to relax for one night and forget about all the bullshit that's going on in your life. Let Arnelle worry about your mom. Let your team handle DQS Cosmetics. For one second let someone take care of you."

Lisa grabbed Dexter's hand and placed it on her inner thigh. Dexter closed his eyes as he worked his hands higher and higher up her thigh. He liked what she was saying. No woman had ever talked about doing anything for him. She always knew what to say when she wanted to. She bit her lips as he spread her legs apart. Her skin felt so soft and warm against his fingers, as he worked his hands up her skirt and slid her thin panties to the side in order to get a better view of her pulsating vagina. Lisa thrust her hips forward and let out a soft moan as she caressed his hand under hers, and encouraged him to plunge his hungry fingers into her wet hole. She threw her head back as he slowly rubbed his fingers up and down her slit. Her legs trembled beneath his touch.

Dexter felt a pang of guilt as Phoenix's hurt face from the hotel room entered his mind. What if she wanted to come back to him? If she found out that he had been with Lisa he would never get his chance. Lisa felt Dexter pull away and hopped off the desk and onto his lap.

She grabbed his face in her hands and kissed him passionately on the lips. At first he tried to turn his head away but she would not be deterred. She placed his hands under her skirt and kissed him deeply. "Damn girl," he moaned. He lifted her dress over her head and revealed her erect butterscotch nipples. He hungrily sucked at her breasts and squeezed her petite waist. Lisa couldn't stop whimpering with ecstasy as he devoured her body. In one motion Dexter lifted her from his lap and lied her down on the desk. She was panting as she reached her arms out to him.

"Make love to me Dexter. It's only one night and then I'm gone." Dexter looked over her body that was his for the taking and ripped her panties off. He knew that he shouldn't do it but he couldn't deny his body and like she said it was only one night.

Dexter plunged his face between her legs and hungrily lapped at her vagina as she screamed out. "Take me now Dexter," she said. "I need to feel you inside of me." Dexter hurriedly dropped his pants and rammed his throbbing penis into her. As he thrust in and out of her he tried to drive the images of Phoenix from his mind. Tonight was his night and he was not going to think about her. He grabbed Lisa by her hair and kissed her hard. Lisa submitted under the intensity of his passion. Although there was a hint of violence in their lovemaking she didn't care. As long as Dexter was with her tonight, that meant that it was one less night that he was with Phoenix. Dexter looked deep into Lisa's accommodating eyes with a sense of self satisfaction. If Phoenix wanted nothing to do with him, then he wanted nothing to do with her either.

Chapter Fourteen

Phoenix stepped into the plush white robe that hung next to the shower. As soon as she had arrived at Big City's house he had ordered her to take a shower while he prepared her a hot cup of coffee. Phoenix resisted at first, but he insisted that a shower would sober her up. She reluctantly obliged him and let the warmth of the water wash over her. She was glad she did. Immediately she felt a cloud had been lifted off of her as the hot water shot out onto her hair and body. She gently dried her hair in the mirror and stared at her puffy eyes.

Although Big City had been kind enough to let her stay at his place before she blew all of her money staying at the Soho Grand, she couldn't shake Dexter's pained face at the hotel from her mind. She was beginning to realize that she was being stubborn for no reason and wished that she could be in Dexter's arms at that moment. She checked her phone to see if he had called. The only missed call she had was from Laila. She would have to wait until tomorrow. Phoenix wasn't in the mood to do any explaining at the moment. She just wanted to rest and get her mind and business together before she had her photo shoot.

"Ouch," she said nursing her aching head as she slipped on the large Fearless Entertainment shirt Big City had left for her. Her head was still slightly spinning and she wished she had some coffee in her hand to make it stop. She made her way to the kitchen. "Is this for me?" she said grabbing the coffee on the counter. Big City looked casual in a jeans and a white t-shirt as he stirred some soup on the stove. "Yeah. I hope you don't mind. I made it light and sweet. That's the way I like to drink it." Phoenix smiled as she sat down on the barstool.

"I would never have guessed that you were a domesticated man Big City." Big City laughed. "First of all call me Sean. You are a guest here. While you are a guest you can call me Sean," he said tasting the soup. "That's really good," he said pouring the soup into a bowl. "But you can only call me Sean in the evening, not while we are working," he said sliding the soup towards Phoenix.

"No problem. I will call you Big City in public," she said sipping her soup. "This is delicious. I can't believe you made this."

"Yeah, that's something people don't know about me. I'm like a five star chef. I can cook almost any cuisine known

365

to man. Cooking is just another extension of my creativity. When I entertain I like to have at least one dish that I've prepared if I can. A lot of times I'm too busy, but if I have the time, I try and do at least one. Like the Patti La Belle Mac and Cheese. My version will make you cry. "

Phoenix giggled to herself at the thought of him cooking. "Well, I am definitely impressed. I have to try it out," she said. "Thank you for letting me stay here."

"It's no problem," Big City said sliding into the chair next to her. "I like you. You sounded stressed so I wanted to be there for you."

"Yeah, I am having a hard time with Dexter as you know. It's like he can't understand that I am trying to make a name for myself and work basically. I mean, you remember what it's like to have something to prove right? He just, he just can't understand that," Phoenix said pushing her soup around.

"Of course I do. I'm proving now. Don't get me wrong, but Dexter is old school. He is from a different era mentally. He will do anything to stay on top and he is using every avenue he can to come back. That includes using new talent and keeping his women close."

"I know, but it hurts because I feel that Dexter really loves me."

"I hate to tell you this but I've known Dexter for some time now, and he is not capable of loving anyone but himself. Look at how he did Lisa. He supposedly loved her until you came along and then he just dropped her."

Phoenix rolled her eyes at him. "He said he loved me. He and Lisa were dying off anyway when I came into his

367

life." "Look, all I am saying is a person like me has nothing to gain from your success. I just want to help out and be a friend. It's no secret that I can't stand Dexter. More importantly, I hate to think that he is doing another good woman wrong. I mean I seen him do it to so many woman over the years and I wouldn't be surprised if he was with another woman right now." Phoenix shook her head.

"No I don't believe that. Dexter is not a dog. Maybe in his past but right now he is trying to get his company together and get everything situated with the campaign. Besides he wouldn't do that to us when we have so many things up in the air."

"Then why don't you call him," Big City pushed the phone in front of her.

"No. I don't want to call him right now. We left on bad terms and I don't want to explain to him where I am right now."

"I think you're scared. You're scared to find out if he is with another woman."

Phoenix grabbed her phone and hopped out of her chair. "Thank you Sean for your concern. I'm going to head to bed. I think I need to get some rest and I will see you bright and early at wardrobe. I am not going to call Dexter tonight. I am going to let it be for now and focus on what I am doing. If Dexter wants to find me, he can call."

She kissed him on the cheek and walked off. Big City eyed her petite body as she walked out of the room in the small t-shirt that fell just below her honey colored buttocks. He felt lucky to have her in his house away from Dexter. If she didn't want to let him know where she was he felt he should do the honors.

Big City picked up his phone and dialed. "Yeah man, it's me. Look, I need you to do me a favor. I need you to give Dexter a call and let him know his girl is safe," he laughed into the phone. He hung up and took a sip of his soup. "Damn good," he said. "I should call Top Chef."

Chapter Fifteen

Lisa kissed Dexter deeply as she stood in the doorway and prepared to leave. She was hoping that Dexter would have invited her to stay, but she knew that would have been asking a lot. Lisa looked deeply into his eyes.

"Dexter this night took me back. Being here at your mom's and being here with you was just what the doctor ordered," she stroked his chest. "I know you are going through a rough time, but you definitely don't have to go through it alone you know? You always have me." Dexter looked away and Lisa grabbed his chin. "I mean that. Look at all that has happened and I am still here. I told you that I am not going anywhere. You know that right?"

371

Dexter shook his head. "You should get back to the city. I have some business I need to finish up and head back myself. I appreciate you being such a good friend to me, but I'm good. Right now I am just moving forward with all the things that we planned on putting in place with the company and that is my main focus."

Lisa tried to hide her disappointment as she gave him one final hug. "Well, like I said. You know where I am. I'm not going anywhere. You have pretty much left your mark on me. I mean what is a girl to do after you right?"

Dexter laughed. "I'm sure you will be alright." Lisa gently touched his arm. "Have a good night."

As Dexter watched Lisa's car slowly pull away, a small pang of guilt washed over him. He felt like he had cheated on Phoenix although they were no longer together. It didn't matter to him. This was all the proof that he needed that women were all the same. If Lisa was willing to be his side piece and his mother wanted children, then maybe there would be a way to make everyone happy. He did still have a year that he had to work with Phoenix. She was under contract and he wasn't going to just let her coast through her contract after all that he had done for her. She was going to owe him big time for this opportunity. She wasn't going to be just another woman that was going to come up and use him.

She wanted to play in the big leagues she had no idea how much fun she was going to have. She thought she had a friend in Big City, she was about to find out the hard way how great a friend he was.

As the stylist rubbed bronzer over Phoenix's slender legs at the photoshoot, she couldn't help but notice that she seemed to be whittling away to nothing over night with stress. She stared at her phone. No missed calls. "Dammit Dexter it's like that?" she tossed her phone to the side. This Flashy photoshoot with Big City was going to bring major exposure for her but all that seemed to be running through her mind was how she had betrayed Dexter. Big City popped his head in to check in on her. They had left separately that morning and Big City had looked surprising gentle as he admired her outfit. "Wow, you look sexy as hell." He grabbed her in a big hug. "You're going to make this shoot so hot. Thank you so much for doing it."

Phoenix smiled shyly. "Thank you for having me and more importantly taking care of me. I mean. I would-" she felt herself getting choked up as she thought about where she would be if Big City had not taken her in and became overwhelmed with emotion. He walked over and put her arms around her.

"Don't think about that now. It's all good. This is going to be good for you. Good for your career. So just think about today and let tomorrow take care of itself. Alright?"

"Alright?" she said"

"Good, let's go do this. Let's get busy!" He stood next to her getting his last minute touch ups.

Phoenix put her game face on. She set her lips in her sexiest and most focused pout as Big City squinted into the lens with his diamonds dripping from his wrists, neck and ears. He slid his strong hands around her waist and pulled her closer to him. She couldn't help feeling a little warm as she leaned in close. The photographer felt inspired to show a sexier side of Big City and encouraged Phoenix and Big City to lean into each other as if they were going to kiss. As they leaned in, Big City took the liberty of gently kissing her lips as the photographer snapped away. Phoenix looked into Big City's eyes and had to look away.

"Beautiful guys. You look in love right now," the photographer encouraged.

"Let's do it again," Big City whispered pulling her close.

Phoenix closed her eyes and kissed him deeply. She didn't want it to end but they had to stop when they noticed the photographer stopped snapping. They both smiled.

She wasn't sure what she felt but it didn't feel like danger. It felt different. It felt very different from the man she had seen in the videos and in interviews. The man she saw for a split second was someone else.

"Are we almost done here," she stuttered.

"Is something wrong baby?" Big City asked. "You look like you seen something crazy."

"Can I get a robe please?" she yelled. Phoenix felt like she needed to get out of the room fast. *What is going on with me? Why can't I just be around a man and be professional? No, this is different.* "I'm good. I think I just need to sit down or eat something. We've been going for awhile."

Big City rubbed her cheeks gently with his hands. Phoenix turned her head. "Please, please Sean. Don't do that," she said. "What?" he grinned. "Yo' Rick we got the shot we need right?"

Rick nodded. "I think so. It's hot. Good job guys."

377

Phoenix wrapped her arms tightly around her body. "You cold?" Big City asked rubbing her shoulders. "No, I just need to change and figure out what's next with this whole DQS shit. Check my messages and make sure my contract is cancelled and deal with my living situation and try to figure my life out."

Big City put his finger to her rambling lips to quiet her. "Baby don't worry about all that I told you. I got you. You already know you have a place to stay. Deal with that Dexter shit tomorrow. The other hustle will handle itself. I have to roll out of town anyway for a week. I have to fly to Germany, so, you know, take that time to think about what you have to do. Can I kiss you again?"

Phoenix blushed. This man was like sex walking. "On the cheek." Big City bent down and gave her a slow kiss that linger on her cheek forever. Phoenix breathed slowly. "Ok that's enough," she said pushing him away.

"You sure?" he said. "I got more."

"No. Have a safe flight."

"Remember you have a place to stay if you need it."

"I will be fine City. Thank you though."

Phoenix loved how Big City seemed to let her just handle her business without standing in her way. But he still provided her a safe place to land if she fell. He was turning out to be such a wonderful friend to her.

"No problem," Big City walked off the set as Charmaine the stylist for the shoot handed Phoenix a small package. "Hey, some dude left and told me to give this to you."

Phoenix eyed the small blue Tiffany box suspiciously. Was Dexter trying to win her back with gifts? Why didn't he just call? This was not his style. His ego was too big.

Phoenix walked back to her dressing room to change rubbing the box surreptitiously in her hands. She sat down in the big fold out chair and opened it. It was a diamond tennis bracelet. *Congratulations, W.D.* Phoenix dropped the box to the floor. This surely could not be from who she thought it was from. But how did he find her? Where was he? What did he want from her after all this time?

Phoenix placed the bracelet back in the box. She was unsure what to do with it. What she did know was that if he thought that buying her jewelry was going to lure her back after all the things that he did to her and after all the years she spent with him, he had another thing coming. She was not going to be bought by anyone especially not Walter.

As Phoenix set the box to the side she couldn't help but wonder if she was doing the right thing by not accepting help from the men that wanted to help her. Who was she kidding? Her whole existence was based on the help of men.

As Phoenix was sitting with the reality of this whole ordeal she was beginning to feel the all too real and sobering feeling that she was not going to be able to perpetrate the life that she had wanted to for so many years. As she looked around at all the clothes and baubles that surrounded her she wondered what it was all really for. She knew that if she had made this career and achieved success on her own that she probably never need a man to give her the things that she thought she needed before. However, with things taking so long to settle and come together as she had wanted them she was beginning to feel a little anxious.

It seemed every time that she was feeling secure enough to handle things on her own a dashing man, her Prince Charming would come into her life and sweep her off of her feet promising her a short cut to fame and fortune or at least a little relief. Yet, it never seemed to work out that way. There actually were no shortcuts. And she wasn't looking for one. Maybe what she was looking for was really love. If not, why did she keep letting it get in the way? After all the things that Walter had put her through Phoenix was surprised that he even had the guts to try to win her back. It took her so long to finally get over the damage that he had done. Yet she knew because of the years he had been in her life that he would always know certain ways to get at her, but not this time she felt strong and determined.

She left the box on the dressing table. Maybe an assistant would find it, or even someone dishonest. She was just going to have to step out on faith and leave her man dependency behind. Phoenix finished dressing and looked in the mirror and smiled at her reflection. She was truly beginning to like what she saw. She just hoped that she would be able to carry that same confidence into her meeting with Dexter tomorrow. She dreaded the moment, but if she was going to be a professional she was going to have to learn to put certain emotions behind so that she could handle her business. She was growing tired of being whatever men projected onto her. She wanted to be more. She wanted to have something to give but she didn't think that beauty was going to be the thing that she had to offer.

Something was telling her that this quest was bigger than just a quest for her career but a quest for herself. She knew that after she had crossed Dexter that there was a huge possibility that her budding career and her contract could be headed straight down the drain. That was something that she was willing to risk for her only chance to prove that she could make something of herself on her own.

Chapter Sixteen

Laila stared coldly at Jacob's dark chiseled body as he stood up from the bed and began to button his shirt. She sighed and handed him his pants. She was finding it harder and harder to let him go on the weekends. She knew they had already discussed that he had to be home for his daughter's birthday party but he already said that it was going to be a real headache standing next to Sheila and the rest of the family pretending that they had something. "With you I don't have to pretend," he'd say. Laila felt like she had been busting her ass for four years to give the same kind of place where he could feel just as financially comfortable and stable like he did with Sheila. How come he couldn't look around and see that they could have a wonderful life here in Brooklyn? How successful was she going to need to get?

"Jacob, don't go. Not right now. Just, stay a little longer. Please," Laila said. "I- I need you baby. I don't want to be alone tonight. I don't want to be alone anymore."

Jacob sat back down and looked lovingly but firmly into Laila's eyes. "Baby you know that I have to go. Whether it's now or an hour from now or two hours from now, I still have to leave."

"But why, when you say that you want a life with me? I mean, what's up with that shit? It's been four years."

"Laila, I keep telling you. It's not about anything but my daughter. I don't want her to grow up without her father. You know as well as I do how that is on a little girl. It's not good. I want to be there," he caressed her cheek. "I don't

386

want to lose you, but, I will understand if you found a better man. You should let him love you the right way. I just want to remain a part of your life."

The tears fell from Laila's eyes as she looked away from Jacob. She wanted so desperately to get out of this situation but she couldn't bear the thought of being all alone without him and starting all over again.

Laila reached over and grabbed her pack of cigarettes. She brought one to her lips and lit the match. Jacob tried to snatch it away but she quickly pulled it from him.

"Stop it Jacob," she said wiping her eyes. "Don't come over here and try to regulate what I do. Especially when you're not even going to be around."

Jacob held his head in his hands. "Please be patient with me. Baby, I got a kid."

Laila shot him a look that made him sit straight up. "Jacob, I have been more than patient with you. I'm almost 30. When am I supposed to start a family? I just feel like I want to get out of this. I have built a fairly successful career; you'd think I'd be smarter about my relationships but obviously not. I just can't." She looked over at Jacob who had inched his way over to the door and put on his jacket. He had a look of sadness and regret in his eyes.

"I have to leave now Laila. I will call you tomorrow. I hope you feel better."

Laila ran to the window to watch as he exited the building.

"Don't call me tomorrow Jacob. I mean it! I will not be here for you," she yelled at his retreating back.

She shut the window and ran to her phone. She had always wanted to call Sheila and tell her that she and Jacob were in love. She thought better of it and threw the phone. She didn't want to upset Jacob. She was tired of living this life and having her man sleep with another woman. She ran over and picked up the phone. Her fingers trembled as they hovered over the keypad. She breathed in deeply. Don't think just do she said to herself.

She quickly dialed Jacob's house. Her heart was pounding in her chest and seemed to beat all the way up to her throat when she heard the gentle voice of Jacob's wife over the phone. "Hello? Hello? Is anyone there?" Sheila said. Laila froze. She wasn't expecting to hear that sound.

Chapter Seventeen

Dexter felt extra light on his feet as he got ready this morning. He had to admit he was feeling a bit of anxiety mixed with anticipation at the thought of seeing Phoenix. It had been nearly a week and although he had been consistently screwing the brains out of Lisa, Phoenix kept crossing his mind. He knew she was staying with Big City and wondered if she was spending nights screaming his name like she had done so many times for him.

The thought alone was enough for him to change the terms of her contract and have her work for pennies. Or better yet, cut her out completely. But he wasn't going to do that. He wanted her around. Cutting her off was not an option, but changing the terms of her contract was. Dexter also knew that she wouldn't protest because she wanted the contract too badly. He knew that she was so blind for fame and success that she couldn't see anything else. If she was ready for the flashing lights he was going to serve up the fast life to her as much as possible. He entered the DQS offices giving a cool wave to his secretary June.

"Mr. Stiles. Ms. Mitchell has been waiting for you in the boardroom," she informed him. "She's not looking too happy either." Dexter smiled to himself. "Thank you."

Dexter entered the boardroom with a cocky grin and sat at the head of the conference table. He stared at Phoenix without saying a word. She looked solemn sitting across from him in a form fitting white dress.

He wanted to walk over to her and throw her across the desk and make her submit to him and apologize but instead he just coughed.

"Need some water Dexter? I've been fortunate to have a few of your bottles while I was waiting past an hour for you," Phoenix said.

"How many bottles did you have?" he asked.

"Four why?"

"Because they are expensive and I wanted to make sure that we account for them on your bill. Those waters are for guests not employees. Of which you are the latter. Keep that in mind the next time you are thirsty sweetheart. I'm writing the checks for everything."

Phoenix could tell where this was going and didn't want to go there with him today.

"Dexter, do whatever you feel. I was hoping that we could get the meeting started. That is if you don't have anything else that you wanted to discuss."

"You have somewhere else to be? Have to get back to Big City?"

"Dexter-"

"I'm impressed. He's got a contract for you? Is he trying to do business or add you to his list of conquests?" he said looking her up and down.

"Alright Dexter, enough. Are we still doing business or not? We've already done test shoots. You have already introduced me to the public. Do you really want to retract all that money you put into marketing me? What about the investors? What would they say? You are doing this over a nonexistent lover's quarrel?"

With that statement Dexter was up and out of his seat and standing over her. "Look, don't you check me. I check you. You work for me. Understand? I work for no one. If I want to throw a new bitch on a billboard tomorrow I'll do it. There are a million of you out there."

Dexter pressed the button on the intercom. "Jane get in here and bring me that updated contract for Phoenix please." Jane immediately burst in with the papers in hand and quickly handed them to Dexter, and slipped out quietly.

He slid the sheets in front of her and handed her a pen. "The items in this contract are non-negotiable. Sign."

Phoenix glanced at him and then the document.

"Dexter what is this? These figures are significantly less than we agreed upon. Why?"

"Well the investors didn't think you were a name talent and lost a little confidence in how the product would sell. They changed the terms with me so I had to change them with you. It's a good deal. For you."

Phoenix eyeballed the contract in her hands. The thought of becoming the face of DQS Cosmetics weighed heavily on her. She knew if she signed the contract she would be forever beholden to Dexter and his demands. She looked up at him to see signs of the man she loved. His face was cold and calculating as he sat with his head cocked in expectation.

"I don't know Dexter," she said. "We had a deal."

"We do have a deal. This deal is actually a more appropriate one. It's one that I would get for any of my clients that were just starting out. I told you that the investors thought that taking a shot on you was a huge gamble. Now, the contract accurately reflects that. I'm not trying to screw you I just want to do business with you. Regardless of what transpired between you and me, I still believe in the woman that walked into my office that first day."

"Really?" she said standing up. "I know you will never believe this but-"

"Mr. Stiles you have an urgent phone call on line one," Jane burst in the door yelling.

"Tell whoever it is I am in a meeting," he said.

"Sir, it can't wait!"

"Give me a moment," he said walking towards the door.

"Dexter, I love you," Phoenix said. Dexter stopped and turned around. Her words hit him like fiery darts.

"Don't play with me Phoenix."

"I'm serious. I am in love with you. He never touched me. I can prove it," she said grabbing the contract ripping it up. "All I could think about when we were apart was how much I loved you. None of this stuff matters."

"Do you know what you're doing right now Phoenix?"

"Yes Dexter I do. I'm doing what makes me happy."

He walked over to her and kissed her deeply.

"Phoenix you have no idea how happy this makes me. I knew from the moment I saw you that I wanted you to be my wife. Promise me you're foreal?"

"I'm very foreal," she nodded.

"Mr. Stiles, the phone. Please," June cried.

"Alright June. I'm on my way," he yelled over his shoulder. He looked back at Phoenix. "You stay right here. I meant what I said. I wasn't prepared for this but I do want you to be my wife. That's what would make me very, very happy."

Dexter rubbed Phoenix's cheek. "I'll be right back. Be naked when I return."

Dexter went into his office and shut the door. "This is Dexter," he breathed into the phone.

"Dexter. Where the hell have you been?" Wade cried on the other line. It was hard for Dexter to understand him through his tears.

"Wade. Calm down. I can't understand you. What's going on with mom?"

"I found her on the floor unconscious this afternoon and called the ambulance."

Dexter's put his hand to his head. "Why was she out of bed?"

"I don't know. It's bad. You need to get here now. Right now. To the hospital."

His mind was racing. He hung up the phone. "June, get me a car right now. I have to leave. Tell Phoenix I had to run out."

Dexter quickly raced around the room to grab some items to take with him. He darted towards the door. "I forgot my phone," he said reaching for the vibrating device on his desk.

"What is it," he said.

"Hey," Lisa said from the other end. She was crying uncontrollably.

"Listen, Lisa now is not a good time. I can't-"

"Dexter, I'm pregnant. Don't hang up."

Dexter dropped the phone and ran out the door.

"Dexter? Dexter are you there?" Lisa asked. "Hello?"